DRAGON
FOR HIRE

Barbara Brooks Wallace

Dragon for Hire

First Pangea Press edition.

An imprint of Pangea
Dana Point, California 92629
ISBN: 0-9894065-5-5
ISBN-13: 978-0-9894065-5-0

FOR VICTORIA AND ELIZABETH

AND DRAGONS EVERYWHERE

.

Table of Contents

NO IMAGINATION

Morris knew that when his fifth-grade teacher, Miss Picklesticker, held up two sets of papers as if they were precious crown jewels on loan from the King or Queen of England, that neither one of the papers was his. He knew it because there was no way in the world that anything he had written would have her special giant A plus written in bright purple ink on top of the first page.

"As you know, class," said Miss Picklesticker, "I had asked you to write a short story or essay stre-e-e-etching your imaginations." She held out her thin arms as far as they could reach with the precious papers dangling from her fingers.

"You also know," she went on, "that I only give one A-plus on any project. But this time there are two papers that have earned it, the papers of Mortimer Quintillius Gribble and Serena Sophronia Gerrelle. I will post them both on our bulletin board, so all of you can see what imagination is all about. Would someone like to help me tack them up, please?"

It seemed that nobody was anxious to help tacking up Mortimer's and Serena's great papers except Mortimer and Serena, who were Miss Picklesticker's pets. Morris knew that anyone else in the class, including himself, would have been embarrassed enough over all this to crawl under their desks, but not Mortimer and Serena. They managed to look like a pair of cats who had just proudly swallowed a pair of canaries as they trotted up to the bulletin board.

Morris (as in Morris Doubleday Clipper) had no intention of going anywhere near those stories, much less reading them. If he were ever going to stre-e-e-e-etch his imagination, it would not come from reading stories written by the likes of Mortimer and Serena. What they had written he didn't care to know, and never would. The papers could hang there on the bulletin board until they grew yellow and their corners curled up, and he would not go near them. Not ever.

The fact was, though, that even if he did break down and read them, it wouldn't do him any good. He had no imagination to stre-e-e-e-etch. Not the tiniest smidgen of one. None at all. Zip. Nada. He had never had any. Not ever.

Morris knew that he had no imagination despite having a mother who wrote highly original "how to" books, and a father who had invented some kind of *thingamawidgets* and made piles of money from manufacturing them, and even a younger sister, Clorinda, who dreamed up make-believe movies in which she was, naturally, the star.

As for the story or essay in which he was supposed to stre-e-e-e-etch his imagination to please Miss Picklesticker, what he had ended up writing about was the cereal he had eaten for breakfast that morning, corn flakes, and how it had compared with the cereal he had crunched the previous morning, which was frosted corn flakes. And the frosted was crunchier because it was covered with sugar, which also made it sweeter. YAWN! He couldn't even make a decent-sized paragraph out of it, much less fill a page. Miss Picklesticker had to str-e-e-e-etch just to give him a C-minus.

Morris thought it was unfortunate that Miss Picklesticker knew all about his high-imagination parents. She would naturally figure that any child of such parents would be dripping with imagination.

Miss Picklesticker probably thought the fairies must have just dropped him on his parents' doorstep by accident, and they took him in out of the kindness of their hearts. This thought actually showed some degree of imagination, but not enough to do him much good.

Morris liked mathematics. That was taught by Mr. Fostersill. In mathematics two plus two made four. You could not imagine it into being five or seven or ten. It was four. Period. No imagination needed. In fact, if you decided to use your imagination in Mr. Fostersill's class, you would get a big fat zero, and no amount of imagination could change that.

Mr. Fostersill was probably as old as Miss Picklesticker, which was going on "pretty darned old," as everyone in the small town of Wister Wibbles said. After all, they had both been teaching at Wister Wibbles Grammar and Middle School since most of Wister Wibblians had been students there, including Morris' mother and father. That, of course, is how Miss Picklesticker came to have her opinions about imagination-less Morris.

Wister Wibbles Grammar and Middle School was a small school in a very small town, but it had advanced with the times. It now had among other things a new red tile roof and an actual basketball court, not to mention such things as water fountains with real water, and toilets that actually flushed every time you flushed them.

However, despite all the changes in the Wister Wibbles Grammar and Middle School, Miss Picklesticker still wore the same two dresses over and over again, the grey one with the blue roses on it on M-W-F, and the green one with the lace collar and cuffs on it on T-TH. Mr. Fostersill's elbows had practically made their way right through the grey sweater that he wore the most. The two of them must have simply preferred looking like old crumpled paper grocery sacks.

Morris liked Mr. Fostersill, and Mr. Fostersill liked Morris, but didn't embarrass Morris or anyone else by making pets out of them. He didn't seem to approve of having teacher's pets. Morris sometimes wondered if Miss Picklesticker actually didn't approve of it either, but just couldn't help herself and had them anyway. He had the feeling they had probably never discussed anything as deep as the subject of classroom pets, or discussed much of anything.

"Good morning, Miss Picklesticker," Mr. Fostersill always said when he passed her in the hall.

"Good morning, Mr. Fostersill," Miss Picklesticker would reply.

This had gone on for years and years. Nobody had ever once heard them address each other by their first names. Nobody actually knew what they even were. So it seemed that they would never have discussed the matter of imagination. Mr. Fostersill could not have had any interest in it, and if Miss Picklesticker had tried to suggest that two plus two could be imagined into something other than four, who knows what kind of mess that would have got them into. Therefore, Morris could believe that they had probably never discussed the subject of imagination, or in his case, the lack of any. one text here.

THE CLIPPERS

Morris' family, the Clippers, lived in a house not too far from the school. Wister Wibbles (Pop. 3, 375 1/2 which would become 376 after Mrs. Doobles produced her fifth baby) may have been only a couple of hours away from a glass-and-chrome-and-taxi-and-tall-building-and-fancy-shop city, but it remained a very small town with a two-block business district, and with mostly very dinky, if not seriously dinky, little cottages.

Morris' parents had started out very, very poor, and had not much more than a shoestring between them when they got married. They borrowed money from the Brinkley's, Morris' mother's parents, who didn't really have very much to loan, and bought the smallest, most run-down, and dinkiest cottage in Wister Wibbles, one that had stood vacant for years because it was too small even by the usual Wister Wibblian standards.

"Wouldn't it be wonderful," they told each other, "if underneath all the overgrown weeds and shaggy vines and spindly branches of sad little excuses for trees we might somehow uncover a nice surprise."

But it turned out to be nothing but a little frame house with peeling paint and filthy, cracked windows. What they saw was what they bought. Not a single nice surprise to be found.

Morris' mother started writing her how-to books on a table squeezed into the tiny broken-down kitchen, and his father Forester started monkeying around with *dingbats* and *thingamabobs* in the dilapidated little garage that was barely big enough to squeeze in a very small car, which they didn't have anyway.

Then Morris' mother sold her first "*how to*" book (it was *HOW TO LIVE ON A SHOE STRING,* naturally), and his father came up with the perfect *thingamawidget,* and got someone with enough money to develop it. Soon pots and pots of money came pouring in.

Now Morris' father went everyday by bus to the big city. There he rose up in a glass-and- chrome elevator to the very top of a tall glass-and-steel building to a big fancy office with soft rugs and comfy leather chairs and an enormous gleaming desk that all looked out through a big shiny window onto another building just as splendiferous as the one he was in. If he wanted a cup of coffee, there were at least ten people happy to run and get it for him. "Lots of cream, no sugar, please."

But every night he still returned to Morris' mother, his sisters Belinda and Clorinda, and Morris in their cozy, but dilapidated, little cottage in Wister Wibbles.

Then Morris' parents started dreaming of buying one of the grand mansions going up in a development some miles from Wister Wibbles called Dibble Dale. They thought about it and talked about it, but being Wister Wibblians to the core, when push came to shove, they couldn't bring themselves to sign on the dotted line of the contracts shoved under their noses by the thrilled real estate lady, Ms. Flipper from Dibblederry, Doublederry, Dabblederry and Derryderry, which was the Dibble Dale sales agency.

"How could we leave Wister Wibbles in favor of Dibble Dale?" they asked themselves. "How could we leave our dear little first cottage? But most especially, how could our children not attend Wister Wibbles Grammar and Middle School, and miss out on Miss Picklesticker and Mr. Fostersill?"

Poor Ms. Flipper suffered a collapse when they decided that instead of buying a house in Dibble Dale, they would keep their dear little cottage, and just add on to it. They did give her a big box of chocolates in an elegant gold foil box, though.

Then they began to add all sorts of rooms, to their cottage, but one thing they added especially was extra garages for Morris' father to tinker in.

It was these garages, all four of them spread out, that were the cause of what happened to Morris, who had no imagination.

Dragon For Hire

WHAT WAS IN THE GARAGE?

"Bong!"

Morris woke with a start. The "bong" from the grandfather clock outside his room had never awakened him before. He was pretty certain it was the "bong" that had done it, because after the clock bonged, it always left a little tingle-buzz-hum kind of sound hanging in the air right after it.

This was the grandfather clock that once belonged to Morris' Grampa and Gramma Brinkley, but which now stood in the hall right outside his room. The clock had come along with piles and piles of stuff and junk and furniture and everything else under the sun from the house they gave up when they decided to live a life of leisure with no lawn to mow, snow to shovel, garbage to take out, or meals to cook, and moved into the Happy Holiday Home, whose motto was, *"We Specialize in Happy People and Where Every Day Is a Happy Day.*

Morris turned and tumbled in his bed. He usually had no trouble falling asleep. And he usually had no trouble staying there once he got there. He never had any exciting dreams, because they probably required imagination, of which he had none. So deep, mostly dreamless, sleep was what he always had.

"Bong!" went the grandfather clock. And then "Bong!" and "Bong!" again.

One plus one plus one made three, just like in Mr. Fostersill's' mathematics class. No imagination required. It was three in the morning. The house was dark and silent because everyone else was fast asleep.

"Everyone else" included Percival, nicknamed Putz, the family Beagle who slept on Morris' bed at night. During the day he slept under the desk in his mother's writing room, and feasted off tidbits of Oreo cookies that she absentmindedly handed him all day long while she clicked away on her computer. He was fed diet dog food one measly time a day, but his waistline did not reflect this. Despite all the imagination abounding in the Clipper's home, not including Morris, it was really amazing that no one could figure out why.

Putz was a deep sleeper, too, and woofed his annoyance when Morris began to turn and twist in bed. But when Morris put his feet down from the bed and stood up, Putz was right down at his heels, panting with expectation that they might be going for a walk.

What happened was that, before Morris went to bed, he had remembered that among all the stuff and junk his Grampa and Gramma Brinkley had dumped on them, when they went off to retire and be happy forever at Happy Holiday, was an old blue-and-red tin truck from Grampa Brinkley's childhood. Grampa had always said that one day Morris should have it when he, Grampa, no longer played with it.

Morris had decided that after school the next day, he would go out and see if he could find it in one of the two newest garages where all his Grampa and Gramma's stuff and junk had been temporarily dumped. His mother and father had said that as soon as she finished her latest "how-to" book, *HOW TO MAKE FANTASTIC GIFTS FROM CLOTHES PINS, PAPER CLIPS, AND WAX PAPER*, and he had put the finishing touches on his new *thingamadoodles*, which was actually an extension of the original *thingamawidgets*, they would go over all the stuff and junk with a fine-tooth comb, and then would hold a gigantic, enormous, knock-your-socks-off Wister Wibbles yard sale.

But what if there was some terrible mistake, and Grampa's tin truck slipped through the fine-toothcomb and ended up in the yard sale? Morris must have been thinking about this when he went to bed. And there was something else.

The new garages had automatic doors, and they had a bad habit of not working. All Morris' father's precious original *thingamawidget* tools and the new ones for his *thingamadoodles* were tightly locked up in the old garage. But most of Gramma and Grampa's stuff and junk was in the newest one, where the door was stuck wide open and refused to close. The garage-door fix-it man couldn't come until the end of the week, maybe not even then. That night, the doorway was still wide open. Anybody could walk right in and help themselves to Grampa's red-and-blue tin truck that was to be Morris'.

So it didn't take much of a "bong" from the grandfather clock to wake Morris all the way up when he must have been hovering near wide-awake-ness from the time he went to bed. But now, what was he going to do about it? Rambling around in their spread-out house in the dark at three in the morning was somewhat on the scary side. But then he wouldn't be in the dark, not entirely, anyway. He would have his super-sized, best-Wister-

Wibbles-Hardware-Store, wide-beam, no-fooling flashlight with him, and for protection, Putz, who not only had a super-sized waistline, but also a super-sized bark. So Morris put on his socks, sneakers, and red-blue-and-yellow plaid bathrobe, and started out with his flashlight in his hand and Putz at his heels.

It was a warm going-on-spring night, and a shiny full moon shone down on Wister Wibbles, painting the whole little town a shimmering silver. Morris didn't even need his flashlight once he stepped through the back door leading to the garages. He turned it on at once, though, as soon as he arrived at the last garage, the one with the door wide open. It was pretty dark inside, and he had no idea where to start looking for his Grampa's tin truck. He stood at the door for a moment, and then started in.

Then all at once Putz stopped and gave a throaty deep growl. Morris looked down and saw the hair standing up on Putz's neck. Amidst all those big dark shapes in the garage, something must be hiding.

If Morris had any imagination, he might have imagined that one of the trunks or boxes was a big black bear from the forest up the road from Wister Wibbles. Only he didn't imagine that. Not exactly, anyway. He only knew it was *something* that wasn't one of Gramma and Grampa's trunks or boxes, and Putz wasn't happy about it.

All at once, he had the thought that maybe looking for Grampa's tin truck wasn't such a good idea after all.

"C-c-come on, Putz!" he whispered in a shaky voice.

But Putz just stood there and started to growl.

Now Morris was truly, seriously, honest-to-goodness, no doubt about it scared.

"Putz, we've *got* to go!" he said.

But Putz wouldn't budge, and Morris wasn't going to leave him behind.

Now Putz started to bark.

One of what looked to Morris like just some big shape in the far corner moved and seemed to get bigger. At the same time, it gave what sounded a like a huge yawn.

"Would you mind getting your animal to shut up," said the shape in a strange, gravelly voice. "He's going to wake up the whole neighborhood. I came in here for privacy. So, if you don't mind."

The shape grew even larger as it stood up.

Morris shone his flashlight on it, and it seemed to grow even larger still, and... and... and spread out what actually looked like wings. Wings! Morris then ran his flashlight over them and yes, that's exactly what they were, wings.

What was this creature? Was it a man in a crazy Halloween costume? It certainly didn't look like a man, and besides, it wasn't even close to Halloween. Was it a bear from that forest outside Wister Wibbles? But bears don't have wings. How about a great, big, huge, enormous bird, like an eagle? But there wasn't even an eagle that big. No, what this creature looked like was nothing more nor less than a... a... a... dragon. A dragon, for Pete's sake!

Now Morris had seen pictures of dragons and even read books that had dragons in them. But he knew dragons were simply mythical beasts. There was no such thing as a real, honest-to-goodness, bet-your-last-dollar-on-it dragon. So he knew, naturally, that he was just imagining this creature. Except that there was just one teeny tiny, teensy weensy, itsy bitsy problem with this line of reasoning. Morris had no imagination. None at all. Zip. Nada.

"I know what you're thinking," said the dragon. "You think I'm a figment of your imagination. Right?'

"W-w-wrong," stammered Morris, who wasn't totally sure what a figment was, but had a pretty good idea. "I have no imagination. I never have had. None at all, Zip. Nada. Miss Picklesticker, my teacher knows it. My mother and my father know it. My sisters know it. Putz my dog doesn't know it, but he's probably the only one in the whole world who doesn't."

"That's a pretty sad track record, but I guess we have to assume that you're not imagining me, and I'm a real honest-to-goodness, bet-your-bottom-dollar-on-it dragon. Right?" said the creature who definitely looked like a dragon.

"I... I guess so," said Morris.

"Well, yes or no?" said the dragon. "Guessing isn't good enough."

"All right then, yes," said Morris. After all, something that looked like a dragon, and said he was an honest-to-goodness, bet-your-bottom-dollar-on-it dragon, and not a product of somebody's imagination who didn't even have one, probably was. A dragon, that is.

Now, one thing about Morris was that, although he might not have had any imagination, he did have one very nice quality that hardly anyone appreciated. He pretty much accepted things as he found them. If he saw someone putting ketchup on their ice cream, or wearing a tie with their tee shirt to school, or one red and one green sock on the same day, he never questioned it. Live and let live was the way it was with him. Therefore he was quite able to accept at once that this was an honest-to-goodness, bet-your-bottom-dollar-on-it dragon. But he did have a lot of questions about it. One particular one, the first one, might not be very polite, but he really felt the dragon owed him an answer.

"What are you doing in our garage?" he asked. Well, what if this so-called dragon had come in there to snitch the tin truck that was to belong to Morris? Okay, so what if?

Dragon For Hire

TOM

"I will be happy to answer that question and any other," replied the dragon. "But first, would you mind turning off that torch you're carrying. There's perfectly good moonlight shining in here, and that thing is ruining my eyes."

Morris turned it off.

"Thank you," said the dragon. "Now, would you explain Putz, please? He makes me nervous. Is he really necessary?"

"Yes he is. And... and... he's a pretty good a-a-attack dog," said Morris. Putz, of course was no such thing. He'd never attacked anything or anyone in his life. But Morris thought it was a good idea to have the dragon think this.

"Oh, I see," said the dragon. "And he's a noisemaker as well. I'm glad he's decided to shut up. He could wake the whole neighborhood. But don't worry; he doesn't need to bother attacking me. I'm quite harmless, I assure you."

"As for the matter of what I'm doing here, well, the door was conveniently open as I flew by. I was looking for a place to stop over until tomorrow night, and this looked as good as any. I wasn't planning to stop this early. But,

17

hey, a place to crash is a place to crash. I thought I'd better take advantage of it. Of course, it was a little early to go night-night, or as in my case, day-day, so I knew it was going to ruin my shut-eye tomorrow. Dragons are night people. I don't suppose you knew that?"

"I didn't," replied Morris. "Actually I don't know much about the habits of dragons. I just know they are dangerous. At least they are in all the stories I've read."

"Forget the stories," said the dragon. "Well, okay, I have to admit most dragons are dangerous. But I happen to be one of your non-dangerous varieties."

"Where do you come from?" Morris asked. "I thought dragons lived in caves in high mountains. We don't have any around Wister Wibbles."

"Is that the name of this place?" asked the dragon. "Well, actually, you're right about the caves in high mountains. I don't come from one anywhere even close to here."

"Which one?" asked Morris although he really didn't know one mountain from another.

"I can't tell you that," said the dragon.

"Is it a secret?" asked Morris.

"Yes, of course," said the dragon. "If you can't tell someone something, that makes it a secret, doesn't it? But I can at least tell you why it's a secret. Are you interested in that?"

"Sure," said Morris, who was *very*. Interested, that is.

"First," said the dragon, "you have to understand that every dragon in the world wouldn't fit into one cave even if they all wanted to. Furthermore, there are many different kinds of dragons. They split into groups way back at the beginning of time and each group has its own cave or clusters of caves. But good, bad, or just plain nasty, all dragons have one code they all follow. Don't tell anyone where a dragon's cave is, yours or anyone else's. It spells danger with a capital D."

"Why?" asked Morris, who wouldn't have entered a dragon's cave for his life.

"You can't guess?" said the dragon.

"No," replied Morris. "You forget... no imagination."

"Sorry," said the dragon. "Well, it's this way. Tell people where the dragons hang out, and first thing you know, people would be out dragon hunting in force. Next thing you know, they'd have a dragon exhibit at every zoo in the world. And what a waste of space!"

"Why?" asked Morris.

"Because let's face it," said the dragon, "who really wants to look at scaly, spiky, slimy dragons when there are, for instance, cute, cuddly panda bears in the same zoo? Most dragons even smell terrible, although I humbly admit my breed gives out a rather nice bouquet of cinnamon and nutmeg. Had you noticed?"

"Sort of," said Morris, who had in fact noticed that the garage didn't have its usual damp dusty smell when he came in.

"To go on," said the dragon, "Your alligators might think they're something special, but we dragons have no illusions about ourselves. It would be a waste of perfectly decent dragons, as well as a waste of space to keep them. Does that answer your question?"

"I guess so," said Morris. "But what are you doing here? I mean, you said you were looking for a place to stop. Stop going where, and to do what?"

"I might ask you the same question," said the dragon. "Do you always go prowling about at night with your noisy dog Putz?"

Morris hesitated.

"Come on, come on!" said the dragon. "I won't tell anyone."

"Well," said Morris, "my Grampa left me a tin truck with all their stuff here when he and Gramma moved into Happy Holiday Home to be happy forever. The garage door is busted and won't come down, and I got worried someone would come and take my truck. I thought I'd better come and get it before anyone else did."

The dragon reached behind himself with a clawed foot and held something out to Morris. "Could this be it? It's been poking me in the behind ever since I got here."

Morris reached out v-e-e-e-ry carefully and took the truck.

"Wow! Gee, thanks!" he said.

"Don't mention it," said the dragon.

Then Morris finally realized something. He knew how the dragon came to be in their garage. But there was still a question more important than that. Much more important.

"You... you said you didn't want anyone to know where you've come from," he said. "But you haven't said what you're doing here anyway. Are you lost?"

"Not really," said the dragon. "I'm here on a mission, if you must know, and I'm looking for possibilities."

"Are you allowed to tell what the mission is?" asked Morris.

"Oh, sure," said the dragon. "I was hoping to find someone to help me with it, and you might be the one. My finding this place to stop, and you showing up is serendipitous, if you know what I mean."

Morris didn't, but he was willing to take the dragon's word for it.

"First, though," said the dragon, "we'd better introduce ourselves. Your noisy dog is Putz, but what should I call you?"

"Morris," said Morris.

"Well," said the dragon, "How do you do, Morris. My name is Tom."

Tom? Who did the dragon think he was kidding? Lack of imagination aside, Morris was not such a nitwit as to believe anything as nutty as that.

"It can't be," he said. "No dragon I've ever read about or even heard about is named Tom."

"Sorry," said the dragon, "but that's my name. Take it or leave it. I do know what you're talking about though, but I have to tell you none of the dragons in my group have the usual far-out weird dragon names to which you are probably referring. We all have names like Ed, Bill or Jack. All except our leader. His name is Grackor-blornPew-dirdack-elmendingrun-wormdall-gorcister-flingdip-thongcarrioca-filadrang-fraugwort-gromindrick."

"Would... would you mind repeating that?" asked Morris.

"Yes, I'd mind," replied Tom. "Bad enough to say it once. I'm surprised I even got through it. The rest of us just call him Old Pew, but never to his face. He expects us to use his full name every time we address him. He's very crafty. He knows that by the time almost everyone gets halfway through, they've forgotten what they came to ask him for. As a result, he leads a pretty restful life with not much to do but sit and look at pictures in the clouds and dream up things for the rest of us to do. Which takes us back to that question you asked of what I'm doing here."

"You mean the mission you're on?" asked Morris.

"Exactly," said Tom. "You've read about dragons, but you've never seen any around, right?"

"Right," said Morris. "You're the first one."

"Well, you may not have seen one of us, but we do keep up with the modern world. Recently Old Pew got it into his head that we need to come around and mingle, and improve the tarnished image of dragons by doing a good deed or two. He picked five for the job, and I'm one of them. I don't know where the other four are or what they're up to. But I personally haven't a clue as to any good deed to do, so I decided I needed someone to help me. That's where you come into the picture."

"But how did you happen to pick *me*?" asked Morris.

"Serendipity, like I said," replied Tom. "An open door appears, and then in comes a boy and his noisy, and I might add chubby, dog. And even better, this boy claims he has no imagination, so accepts right away that I am a real honest-to-goodness, bet-your-bottom-dollar-on-it dragon. Anyone else would have probably figured he was having a nightmare, then gone right back to bed."

"True," agreed Morris, "but it sounds like you're expecting me to come up with good deeds for you to do. I can't think of one, and having zero imagination doesn't exactly help. Besides, I don't know a single person who needs a deed done, and don't know how to find one. Maybe you picked the wrong garage and the wrong boy. Don't you think you ought to fly off and look further?"

"No," said Tom. "I'm sure you can think of something if you really put your mind to it. Come on, now, give it a try."

Morris shrugged. "I don't know. All I can think of is something really nutty like putting an ad in the paper." He was thinking at the same time that anyone who answered a nutty ad like that would have to be just as nutty as the person who put it there.

"Bingo!" said Tom. "I figured you'd think of something. A splendid idea! There must be someone out there who needs at least one good deed done."

"Like what?" asked Morris, whose imagination, considering he really had none, had been stre-e-e-etched almost to the breaking point with the nutty newspaper ad idea. "Anyway, what kinds of stuff can dragons do by way of good deeds?"

"We fly, naturally. I could provide cheap transportation for someone," Tom said.

"But what if someone wants to do something more than just fly. How could you do it?" asked Morris.

"I was thinking you'd help me out," replied Tom. "If you wouldn't mind?"

"Depends on what the deed is," said Morris, who didn't really think he'd be called up to do anything in the end because there was no one who would answer their nutty ad. "I'm only eleven, in case you haven't figured that out."

Still, even though Morris was telling himself that this was all pretty crazy, he was actually getting excited about it. What if they put an ad in the paper, and someone answered it who *wasn't* nutty and really needed help? Doing good deeds with a dragon wasn't something many people got to do.

"We'll just have to see what comes up," Tom said.

"But what would we say in the ad?" Morris asked.

"Oh, that's an easy one," Tom said. "Just say *DRAGON FOR HIRE*. That ought to do it."

"Yes," said Morris, "but what if someone wants a deed done that isn't just traveling? Maybe we should add something."

"Like what?" asked Tom.

"Well, like *All Jobs Considered. No Job Too Large. No Job Too Small.*" Morris said. He had just remembered the business cards stuck on their refrigerator of painters and electricians and plumbers his family had used every time they added on to their house.

When he was about seven he had called the paint people and told them he was calling for his mother because she was busy, and would they come out and do a paint job. The paint job, when the painter arrived, turned out to be where Morris' Tinker Toy truck had lost a chip of paint. Nobody was happy about this. Not Morris' mother, not the painter, and in the end, not Morris, who had been given time-out in his room for half a day. From then on, he never believed anything those cards on the refrigerator said.

Still, Tom liked the *No Job Too Large. No Job Too Small* idea.

"You have to promise you mean it," said Morris

"I promise," said Tom.

So they decided to add *All Jobs Considered. No Job Too Large. No Job Too Small* to DRAGON FOR HIRE. But there were still some problems to be worked out, such as putting the ad in the paper.

"I'd be happy to do it," said Tom, "but we both know that wouldn't work."

It didn't take much brainwork to figure that one out. Morris was the one who would have to do it. Then there was the matter of paying for it. Tom confessed with some embarrassment that he hadn't considered needing money. Old Pew hadn't thought of it either, he said.

That was okay, said Morris. He had a pretty full piggy bank, although probably not full enough for an ad in the big city *TIMES*. Anyway, as that would require him to write a check, which he couldn't do, and use a credit card, which he wasn't allowed to have, this would have to be a cash transaction. And on all accounts, that meant an ad in the *WISTER WIBBLES TIMES*. This didn't give them much of a pool to draw from, but it was the best they could do.

He would leave for school early the very next morning, which it just about already was, and stop off at the *TIMES* office downtown, which was a hop and a skip away from Wister Wibbles Grammar and Middle School. If he was lucky, their ad could make the *TIMES* for that evening.

"If somebody answers the ad, how will they do it?" Tom asked. "I don't know how these things work."

"I don't either," said Morris, who had never placed an ad of any kind, and certainly not one advertising deeds done by dragons. "I don't want anybody telephoning here. If whoever answered the phone wasn't me, they'd think it was a wrong number, or somebody escaped from the loony bin."

"Is there a loony bin close by around here?" Tom asked.

"No," said Morris. "But everyone in my family has great imaginations. Who knows what they'd think? It's too risky."

There was silence in the garage for several moments, except for Putz snuffling around in the corner where there was an old television set sitting on an old white enamel kitchen table, one which Gramma Brinkley had once used for rolling out pie crust, and which she said she would never be really happy about having to give up. But the TV on the table in the garage, lit only by moonlight shining through the open door looked like something he had in his room, a table with his computer on top. *COMPUTER!*

Morris had his own computer address. He'd all but forgotten about it because whom did he have to write letters to? Or get letters from? He had to think a moment before he even remembered his computer address *putzinapuddle@cork.com*. But that was the answer.

"Do you know what a computer is?" he asked Tom.

"You've got to be kidding," said Tom. "I wasn't born yesterday. And as I told you, we're pretty much up on everything, and that includes computers. We dragons may not have any, but that doesn't mean we don't know the score. I'd appreciate it if you didn't insult my intelligence further."

"I'll do my best," said Morris. "You have to remember, I've never met up with a dragon before."

"And I've never met up with a boy," said Tom. "That makes us even. But not to get off the subject, what did you have in mind about this computer business?"

"Well, I have a computer, and I'll just put my computer address in our ad," said Morris. *"putzinapuddle@cork.com."*

"Hmmm," hummed Tom. "I don't think much of that address, but whatever works." He gave a huge yawn, giving off a few sparks.

Morris had forgotten all about dragons and fire breathing.

"Watch it!" he said. "There may be some flammable stuff here. Could you cut it out with the sparks, please?"

"Sorry," said Tom. "I was forgetting myself."

"Okay," said Morris, "Anyway, it looks if we've got everything settled. But where are you going to stay while we wait for answers to our ad? I guess you could stay here if you like. The garage door fix-it man isn't coming for a few days. My parents are too busy to clean up all the stuff here right now, which they're going to do for a yard sale."

"Yard sale, eh?" said Tom. "That sounds like fun. You don't suppose... no, I'd better not consider it. Probably put a damper on everything if a dragon was seen hanging around."

"Probably," said Morris. Damper would hardly be the word for what could happen if Tom showed up. Riot, would be more like it.

"Well I'll stay here until then," said Tom. "As I told you, I sleep during the day, and am up at night. I'll just fold myself up behind those boxes in the corner. Will I be seeing you tomorrow night with a report?"

"Oh sure," said Morris.

"I don't suppose you'd bring me something to eat, would you?' Tom asked.

Morris hesitated. What he'd read about dragons and their eating habits wasn't worth talking about. Yuck, actually.

Tom chuckled. "I suppose you've read all that nonsense about dragons eating habits. What did you think?

We only dine on princesses, maidens, damsels in distress, and delicacies like that?"

"Well, don't you?" asked Morris.

"Don't be ridiculous," said Tom. "People write that nonsense when they don't know what they're talking about. It puts dragons in a very bad light, I have to tell you. There ought to be a law against it. Anyway, what have you got to offer?"

It was relief not to have to try to find a princess or something like it languishing in their kitchen, but Morris had to try to remember what they *did* have stored in their pantry. He supposed it would take quite a boatload of food to fill a dragon. He could only think of one thing they had lots of that his mother wouldn't miss.

"How do you feel about cornflakes?" he asked.

Dragon For Hire

MISS PLINKER OF THE WISTER WIBBLES TIMES

Bong! Bong! Bong! Bong! Bong! Bong! Ping!

Morris drowsily heard the grandfather clock strike six thirty. He had actually set his alarm clock for six when he came back to his room at three forty-five a.m. But when his alarm went off, he looked at his clock and couldn't remember why he had done anything so stupid. So he set the snooze alarm, and drifted back off to sleep.

Through a haze, he heard the grandfather clock bonging, opened one eye, looked at his clock, and then something came drifting into his mind, that crazy dream about a dragon in their garage. He also dreamed that he had written something on his computer.

Bong! Seven o'clock now.

He crawled out of bed and padded over to his computer. He really felt stupid. There wouldn't be anything there, naturally. But lying right beside the computer was a note. It was the note he dreamed he had typed, "Ad to take to *WISTER WIBBLES TIMES. DRAGON FOR HIRE – NO JOB TOO LARGE-NO JOB TOO SMALL.* Report to Tom the Dragon tomorrow night."

Beside the computer sat Grampa's red fire truck. How could he have brought that in from the garage and not even remembered that either?

Was it possible that it was no dream? He couldn't have imagined the whole thing because he knew he had no imagination. None at all. Zip. Nada. He decided he must be going seriously nutty, but there was one sure way to find out.

He threw on his socks and sneakers, underwear, and his jeans and Wister Wibbles Grammar and Middle School purple sweatshirt. Putz was leaping around at his heels, expecting to be let out into the fenced back yard. His tail started going a mile a minute when Morris put his leash on. Walkies! But Morris knew his mother would already be in the kitchen making breakfast, especially as she was beginning to work for the very first time on a "how to" cook book, *HOW TO COOK YUMMY BREAKFASTS FROM NOT MUCH IN THE PANTRY*. Putz on a leash would explain why Morris was going out the back door at that hour.

"Where are you going, sweetie?" asked his mother, covered in flour and looking distracted. She had just discovered that it wasn't easy to cook yummy breakfasts from not much in the pantry, and was wondering if there wasn't some other yummy thing it might be easier to make when you had nothing to make it with.

"Going out to see if there's a dragon in our garage," replied Morris, who never lied to his parents.

"That's nice, sweetie," said his mother.

Morris hurried out the back door.

When he and Putz arrived at the open garage door, Putz started whining at some big shape in the far corner. And it didn't look like any old box, either. Furthermore, it gave out the definite smell of cinnamon and nutmeg. Further than that, the shape was definitely breathing. Omigosh! Omigosh! Omigosh! Morris couldn't have dreamed this whole thing up. It really *must* be a dragon. A dragon with a pleasant smell and the idiotic name of Tom. But a dragon, nonetheless.

Putz started to bark.

"Cut it out, Putz!" Morris said, and gave him a sharp tug on the leash to show he really meant it. "It's only a dragon, for Pete's sake. Get a grip, Putz. You two have already met. Come on, we're going back in."

Poor Putz was barely able to take care of his necessary business before he was dragged back into the garage.

And the reason, Morris now knew, why he had set his alarm clock for six-o'clock was because he had to get down to the *WISTER WIBBLES TIMES* before school so their ad would make that evening's edition. After all, Tom only had a few day's use of their garage before the fix-it man came to fix the door, or his parents started giving it the fine-tooth-comb treatment to get ready for the grand yard sale.

Morris didn't have high hopes that the ad would do a lot of good, but it was the only thing they had thought of to find a good deed for Tom, which he could then report to Old Pew. Morris really wanted to be the one to help Tom earn Brownie points with him, or whatever points dragons earned.

It had now become a matter of pride. If Tom didn't do any deeds that week (even one deed would be nice) he might have to go looking for another garage and another boy. Morris wanted to be *the* boy. And there was another thing. What if Old Pew only gave the dragons a few days to do their deeds? Tom would go back to his cave in disgrace. That could not happen!   Morris' sisters always liked to meet up with their girl friends to walk to school, so Morris didn't have to worry about raising any suspicions, if he didn't head right for Wister Wibbles Grammar and Middle School. He stuffed down a bowl of cornflakes just as he always did, and then raced to his room, unlocked his piggy bank, and stuffed a bunch of money into his jeans pocket, just as he always did *not* do. His piggy bank money was being saved for something really special, as yet to be determined. But if helping a dragon do a good deed wasn't special, then what was?

He arrived, panting, at the front door of the *WISTER WIBBLES TIMES* just as a pretty young woman was unlocking the front door. She quickly tripped around behind the counter, turned around a little black-and-gold sign that said *"MISS PLINKER,"* and gave Morris a dazzling smile.

"What can I help you with, sir?" said Miss Plinker.

What can I help you with, sir? And not *shouldn't you be in school, young man?*

It was all Morris could do not to break right down on the spot and tell her all about the help he needed. He was dying to tell *someone*, but he knew he couldn't. Not Miss Plinker, not any friends at school, not his family, and certainly not Miss Picklesticker, even though it might help him to get a C on his next paper, if she believed he was beginning to get goofy thoughts about dragons in garages in his head.

Morris shoved the piece of paper with the ad printed on it across the counter. "I'd like to get this in tonight's edition," he said. "Is it too late?"

More dazzling smiles came from Miss Plinker. "Not at all," she said, counting out the words.

Miss Plinker could have asked if Morris was bringing in this ad for his father or uncle, or even a grown-up friend. Instead, all she said was, "Would you like this in a boxed ad, sir? It won't cost much more, and boxed ads always get more attention."

"How much is it? I mean with the box and everything," asked Morris. He pulled out the bunch of wadded bills he had stuffed into his pocket and dumped them on the counter.

"Oh my," said Miss Plinker. Another dazzling smile. "Not all *that*!"

She carefully pulled out a few bills from the pile, showed Morris what she had in her hand, and handed all the rest back.

"See?" she said. "And you do know the ad will run all week, don't you?"

"I didn't," said Morris. "Wow!"

"Yes, wow!" said Miss Plinker. "THE WISTER *WIBBLES TIMES* really is a bargain."

"It sure is," said Morris. Wait until he told Tom about this! "Now," said Miss Plinker, "How would you like people to reply to this ad?"

"Oh," said Morris, "to my Email address is fine. It's *putzinapuddle@cork.com*,"

"You know," Miss Plinker said, "I don't usually question ads, but...."

Uh oh! Morris thought. What was she going to ask him? He'd better have an answer ready.

"But," said Miss Plinker. "I've never heard of a *Dragon*. What kind of car is that? Is it foreign?"

"Sort of," said Morris, and smiled mysteriously.

"Oh, I see, a secret," said Miss Plinker. "Well, as I suspect you're not quite ready for a driver's license, I hope you have a good driver for your *Dragon*, and gets lots of business."

"Thank you," said Morris.

NIGHT FLIGHTS BY DRAGON

That night Morris set his alarm for two a.m. before he went to bed. He might as well not have gone to bed at all for all the sleep he got. Bong! Bong! He was already out of bed even before the reminder from the grandfather clock.

As he had gone to bed with his clothes on, all he had to do was put on his socks and sneakers before he crept from his room with his super-sized, best Wister-Wibbles-Hardware-Store, wide-beam, no-fooling flashlight. The house was dark and silent, as naturally everyone had long since gone to bed.

Morris also had to take Putz with him again, because Putz would have made such a rumpus if he hadn't that it would have awakened the whole family. He'd better not tell Tom how perilously close he came to doing just that.

Then Morris and Putz went straight to the pantry where all the food was kept that wasn't in the refrigerator.

When Morris' father and mother had started expanding their house, one of the main things they wanted was a huge enormous, you-practically-needed-a-car-to-get-around-in pantry to store not just pots and pans, but boxes and tins and jars of food. "Emergency Food" they called it, although they didn't know what emergency they exactly had in mind.

In the end the old dining room had been turned into a kitchen, and the old kitchen into the pantry. The tiny old kitchen had actually been the largest room in the house, so there it was, the perfect large pantry. It almost seemed as if they had both been starved as children, which wasn't the case at all. They just liked having lots of food available.

"You would think they'd all be walking tubs of lard," said Gramma and Grampa, whose former pretty big house didn't even have such a pantry. "But they are all skinny as beanpoles," Gramma said.

At any rate, it was really lucky that they had the large pantry, thought Morris, now that he had a dragon to feed. Still, he couldn't just go in and ransack the place without raising suspicions. He thought of cornflakes a) because he had just written about them for Miss Picklesticker and got a C minus for his lack of imagination, and b) because despite all that money from the *thimgamawidgets,* his father remembered the shoe string they once lived on, and never passed up a "good deal" when one came his way. In this instance, the "good deal" was two cases of cornflakes, one plain, and one sugar frosted, from his friend Hobart McFiggle, the manager of the Wister Wibbles Greens and Groceries, the main grocery store in Wister Wibbles.

Morris took six boxes of cornflakes, three plain and three frosted, from the back rows. There were some other possibilities, but first he would have to see what Tom would eat, and how much of it. If necessary, as the *TIMES* ad had cost a lot less than he thought, he still had some piggy bank money. He could always load up at Greens and Groceries, provided his father's friend Hobart McFiggle didn't see him doing it.

Clutching the six boxes of cornflakes, his super-sized, best Wister Hardware Store, wide-beam, no-fooling flashlight, and Putz's leash, he tiptoed out the back door to the garage with the open door. The moon was pouring its silver light into the garage. But when Morris looked around, he didn't see any big lump in the back where Tom should have been. Putz was remaining pretty calm as well. Morris quickly turned on his super-sized flashlight and shone it all around the back of the garage. No Tom!

This could only mean one thing. At long last, Morris had developed an imagination! Everything from last night was just one big flaming non-event that he had imagined. This might have been a very good thing that would thrill a lot of people, especially Miss Picklesticker. But his spirits fell with a huge, enormous, rattling, shake-the-garage-right-off-its-foundation thunk. What an idiot he was. Those notes he had typed on his computer and printed out!

That ad in the *WISTER WIBBLES TIMES!* Even valuable money from his piggy bank gone! What an idiot! Worse than that, a raging loony!

And then suddenly Morris heard something behind him, the sound of wings flapping. Putz gave a couple of small "woofs," and Morris whirled around, dropping all the boxes of corn flakes.

There was Tom, skidding to a beautiful landing right outside the garage. He cleared his throat, sending out a few sparks that went dancing across the driveway.

"Sorry about that," Tom said. "That always happens when I do a landing. I'll try to control it. Hello, by the way! I was worried you might start in on that imagination business, decided you actually had one, and never show up."

"Wh…wh…where did you go?" Morris stammered. "I… I thought… I thought…."

"That you actually had imagined me?" said Tom, slithering into the garage. "I really am sorry. I didn't think you'd get here this early. I was just out for a little fly around. *You* know how it is. A fellow has to stretch his wings after a day's sleep. And you can turn that floodlight off now, if that's okay with you."

"Oh sure," said Morris. He now realized he'd been getting a whiff of Tom's left-behind cinnamon-nutmeg smell all along. Putz lay down beside him and put his head on Morris' sneaker. He seemed to be all over his dragon worries.

"So did you get the ad in?" Tom asked.

"I did," said Morris. "A lady named Miss Plinker told me it's going to run all week."

"Good!" said Tom. "You didn't, by the way, tell this Miss Plinker anything about anything, did you?"

"Oh no!" said Morris. "But we can't get our hopes up too high. It's just a newspaper ad and the *WISTER WIBBLES TIMES* is just a dinky little newspaper."

"Well, *que sera sera*," said Tom. "I'll keep my claws crossed. But did you bring me anything to eat? I'm starved."

"Cornflakes," said Morris, handing Tom the boxes.

"I'll give them a try," said Tom. "Nothing else? No princesses? No damsels in distress?" He gave a throaty chuckle, which unfortunately released a few sparks that went skipping across the garage floor.

"Watch it!" said Morris.

"Sorry!" said Tom. He tore open a corn flakes box, and emptied the whole of the contents into his mouth. "Not bad," he said. "But nothing else, eh?"

"I'll try to get something more," Morris said. "How about spaghetti? Mac and cheese? I think we have a lot of that."

"Sounds good to me," Tom said. "But I have to tell you, quantity is almost as important as quality. It takes quite a lot to fill up a dragon."

"I was afraid of that," said Morris. "But I've still got money in my piggy bank. I'll get stuff from the grocers if I have to."

"You know something, Morris," Tom said. "It seems to me all this is about me. What's in it for you? Nothing! It doesn't even do anything for your no-imagination problem."

"Oh, that's all right," said Morris. "It isn't every day that a boy gets to meet up with a real dragon. I'm okay with it. Really."

"Well, I have an idea," Tom said. "How'd you like to meet another dragon?"

"Right now?" said Morris.

"Why not?" asked Tom.

"Cool!" said Morris. "Would you be taking me back to your cave to meet Old Pew?"

"Not on your life!" said Tom. "Besides, you remember what I said. I can't even tell you where my cave is, much less take you there. Old Pew would have me by my spiked tail if I showed up with a boy."

"So who is this other dragon?" Morris asked. "And how come I'm allowed to see where he lives?"

"Well, to begin with," said Tom, "his name is Bert. He's a really nice fellow, but he has this problem. His family won't have anything to do with him, so he's gone off to live on top of a mountain all by himself. I'm not sure I should even be taking you there, but I'll trust you to keep this to yourself."

"Sure," said Morris. "Nobody'd believe me anyway. They wouldn't believe me if told them about *you*, for Pete's sake. So what's his problem, anyway?"

"Fireworks!" said Tom. "He breathes fireworks."

"Fireworks?" asked Morris. "Fireworks like what?"

"Fireworks like Roman candles, pinwheels, twisters, skyrockets, and fountains. You know, just your common, run-of-the-mill fireworks," said Tom.

"Cool!" said Morris, who could see what a wow this Bert would be if he could get him to put on a performance at the Wister Wibbles Park on the Fourth of July. "What's wrong with fireworks?"

"Nothing if it's only sort of a hobby," said Tom. "But he's been doing this since he was a baby. He used to just sit by himself on a rock blowing specks of twinkling lights into the air. He never went swooping around the countryside with his brothers and sisters and the rest of us. His family gave up on him, so when he grew up, he found a place off by himself. I was his friend, so I know where it is. If you like, we'll go drop in on him. See how he's doing."

"Wow!" said Morris. "But don't you want to finish your dinner first?"

"I already have," said Tom, and pointed his foot at five empty boxes on the garage floor.

Crunch! Crunch! Crunch! Crunch! Crunch!

He'd emptied all five while they were talking. "I'm leaving one for a snackeroo before I turn in for the day. What do you say? Shall we take off?"

"What about Putz?" asked Morris.

"Bring him along," said Tom. "I assume he'd behave himself."

"Oh sure," said Morris, sure actually of no such thing. But he could hardly leave Putz wandering around the yard by himself.

Morris wasn't even certain how Putz would enjoy the flight, but hanging on to him as tightly as he could, he climbed aboard Tom's back. He was completely surprised at how soft Tom's back was. It might look scaly, spiky and slimy, but it wasn't anything like that. Or maybe it was just Tom's special kind of dragon. After all, he didn't even have dragon smell, or what you'd think a dragon would smell like, a stagnant pond, or a swamp, or old mildewed rubber galoshes. He actually did smell like a mixture of cinnamon and nutmeg, like spice cookies baking.

"All set?" said Tom.

"All set!" said Morris.

Tom spread his magnificent wings, and off they sailed into the moonlit night sky.

Nobody needed imagination on a trip like the one Tom took Morris and Putz on. There was nothing that needed to be left to the imagination because it was all right there, the stars, the moon, the soft night air, the twinkling streetlights of sleeping Wister Wibbles, and the twinkling all-over lights of the still-awake big city.

Tom dipped and swooped down so Morris could have a close look at what was below. Then up he sailed again. They were like a big ocean-going ship, only they weren't on a ship, and this wasn't the ocean. What it was, was magic.

"Before we go to see Bert, could we look in on my father's office?" Morris asked. "He said some day he'd take me, but he never has."

"How are we ever going to find it?" Tom asked.

"It's the tall building with the big golden globe on top," said Morris. "My father's office is right in the middle of the fifteenth floor he says."

"Okay, you got it," said Tom.

And that's how Morris saw his father's office for the very first time. As Tom hovered outside the window, Morris saw moonlight pouring in on his father's big gleaming desk where he had his coffee (with cream and no sugar), and the big soft leather chairs, and even on one wall the black iron doors with chrome wheels of a huge safe where all the *thingamawidget* secrets were kept (all in code, of course), and piles and piles of money. Of course, Morris knew he could never say he'd already seen it when he was with his father. He would practice looking surprised in front of a mirror before he ever was invited.

"Seen enough?" Tom asked. "You ready to go see Bert? Maybe he'll do some fireworks for us."

"Super cool!" said Morris.

Dragon For Hire

BERT, THE FIREWORKS DRAGON

They arrived at a tall mountain, and Tom began swooping back and forth, back and forth.

"That's funny," he said to Morris. "It's dark as a dragon's insides. No pinwheels, no Roman candles. Nothing!"

"Maybe he's asleep in his cave or something," said Morris.

"Not at this hour of night," said Tom. "This is when he's out doing his thing, so to speak. I'm just going to glide in and park. I don't like the looks of this. Hang on tight, I'm coming in for a landing."

In moments, Tom had swooped down and come to a stop on a ledge high up in the craggy mountain. The moment he landed, Morris could see a big, hulking shadow in the moonlight just sitting there, not moving.

"Hey, Bert!" Tom called out. "What's up, old fellow? Why no lighting-up the night with a couple of skyrockets and fountains? I've brought someone to see you, and I more or less promised him a show. This is Morris, by the way, and his four-legged friend, Putz."

"Well, you can just go away, and take them with you," said a doleful voice. "I'm not interested."

"Come on, this is your old friend Tom," said Tom. "Can't you tell me what's wrong?"

"I'd rather not," said Bert. "You'd better just go. I'm not fit to be your friend, anyway."

"That's the dumbest thing I've ever heard in my life," said Tom. "Come on now, and tell me the problem. It can't be that bad."

"Oh, yes it can," said Bert gloomily. "How would you like to be told you're a disgrace to dragonhood?"

"Who told you an idiotic thing like that?" asked Tom. "You have a great talent, my friend. Just because your family can't see beyond their noses. If you want to know, I think they're all jealous. All we can do is send out the usual dragon run-of-the-mill flames and sparks. They don't compare with those fireworks you produce."

"But this has nothing to do with fireworks," said Bert dismally.

"So what's it all about then?" Tom asked.

"Well, one night a dragon dropped in on me. He wasn't from our cave. Said his name is Glorgrim. You know, the usual dragon kind of name. Not like ours, worse luck. I invited him for dinner and gave him a nice little dandelion salad with fresh mushrooms, and wild berries for dessert."

"Sounds good to me," said Tom.

"*He* didn't think so," said Bert. "Asked me if I didn't have any damsels and maidens and that sort of thing to offer like any other self-respecting dragon. When I told him I didn't, he told me I was a disgrace to dragonhood and left without even finishing his dessert. So there you have it!"

Tom gave a hoot of laughter that sent sparks dancing all over the ledge. "I've heard of that Glorgrim," he said. "He's a total idiot. Where's he been hiding himself? He's living in the dark ages. No dragons go in for that anymore. It's what I told my friend Morris here."

"That's not the worst of it," said Bert. "I went around collecting a bunch of maidens and a couple of damsels in distress. Now I've got them all pining away in my pantry and I don't know what to do with them. They require a lot of upkeep, I can tell you. One day some oddball knight in shining armor came up to rescue them, but he only took one damsel in distress and left the rest. Besides being depressed, taking care of them has worn me out and I'm too tired to give fireworks shows to the poor villagers down below. They've been doing very well selling tickets, and I expect they've had to give the money back."

"Do they know it's a dragon giving these performances?" asked Tom.

"Oh no!" said Bert. "They just think it's a natural phenomenon that's suddenly gone phhhhhht! They're too scared to come up to investigate, which is just as well."

"Excuse me, Tom" Morris whispered, "But why couldn't Bert just take all the maidens and damsels back where they came from?"

"Thank you, Morris," said Tom. "Did you hear that, Bert? My friend Morris is right. That's exactly what you should do."

"And I wouldn't be considered a disgrace to dragonhood if I did that?" asked Bert wistfully.

"Glorgrim is the one who's a disgrace!" said Tom. "If he ever comes around again, tell him so. Don't be such a wimp, Bert. It's just as I told Morris. That sort of nonsense has ruined our reputations. Morris, you and Putz wait here. I'll help Bert empty his pantry. Dining on damsels, what a laugh!" said Tom.

In no time Tom and Bert collected all the maidens, and the one remaining damsel in distress, who was swooning with delight, and flew them back to their homes.

And before Tom took Morris and Putz back to Wister Wibbles, they were treated to one of the most splendid fireworks displays Bert had ever put on.

"Wow!" said Morris as he and Putz winged home on Tom's back. "Do you suppose I can come back some time to the village and see more of Bert's fireworks shows?'

"Sorry," said Tom. "But you know the rules about revealing where dragons live. I probably shouldn't have brought you here in the first place."

"I know, Tom. Thanks!" said Morris.

It had been a very exciting and surprising evening. But Morris had another surprise waiting for him when he returned to his room. He turned on his computer just in case, but was really not expecting anything as crazy as a reply to the *DRAGON FOR HIRE* ad. But he had an e-mail letter, and it was a real, honest-to-by-golly-no-mistaking-it-for-junk-mail letter!

"I would like to have a dragon ride. Please let me know when I can have it." The letter was signed *"FERDY."*

Dragon For Hire

FERDY@KITKAT.COM

The e-mail from Ferdy had come in much earlier that evening, but Morris hadn't bothered to check his computer. He hadn't expected much from the ad in the first place, and certainly not on the very first day it was in. The e-mail must have been sent the minute the *WISTER WIBBLES TIMES* landed on someone's doorstep. Though whoever sent it must have long since gone to bed, Morris decided to answer immediately anyway so this Ferdy would see his reply first thing in the morning. *"Ferdy, thank you for replying to the ad. If all you want is a dragon ride, please be by an open window at the backside of your house tomorrow at one a.m. Also, please send your address. Thank you. Thaddeus Q. Putz, DRAGONS, INC., YOUR TRANPORTATION SERVICE. OTHER JOBS ALSO DONE"*

Morris thought it was clever to add this last as the more deeds Tom could cram in, the more he could report to Old Pew. Ferdy, whoever he was, needed to be reminded that their company could do more than just provide dragon rides. Morris went to bed in a high state of excitement. It's a wonder he got any sleep at all before his alarm went off again at seven.

He knew he wouldn't find a reply to his letter in the morning, but ought to have one when he returned from school. Who could Ferdy be, anyway? Morris hoped he wouldn't mind that it was only a boy who headed up the dragon service appearing at his window. But was it possible that Ferdy thought along with Miss Plinker that "dragon" was the name of a car? More than anything, though, Morris hoped that somebody wasn't just trying to be funny in answering the ad. Well, if that *were* the case, this Ferdy would soon be laughing out of the other side of his face when he saw who was pulling up outside his window!

As soon as he blasted through the front door that afternoon after school, Morris tore up to his room and turned on his computer. There it was, a reply from Ferdy@kitkat.com! *"My address is 1435 Putty Street. I will be at a window in the back at one a.m. Should* I wear *earmuffs? Ferdy*

Earmuffs? Was this Ferdy older than he thought? A *LOT* older. Maybe so old he was getting a little fuzzy in the brain? Why would he think he needed earmuffs, for Pete's sake? But on the other hand, Morris *had* been a little chilly on his ride with Tom the night before. Maybe earmuffs weren't a bad idea. He himself probably ought to wear a jacket over his purple Wister Wibbles Grammar and Middle school sweatshirt. He sent an e-mail right back to Ferdy@kitkat.com.

"Wear ear muffs. Wear warm jacket also. Thank you. DRAGONS, INC., YOUR TRANSPORTATION SERVICE. OTHER JOBS ALSO DONE."

Morris thought it wouldn't hurt to remind this Ferdy again about those other jobs Tom could do. Or maybe what he himself could do, as Tom had pretty much said all he could do was offer flights. Morris would see that Tom got credit for any deed done by himself, as it wouldn't earn any dragon points with Old Pew, if he had to admit it was

Morris who actually did the deed. Morris was pretty sure Tom wouldn't lie about that.

Morris only hoped his mother wouldn't stay up late as she sometimes did to work on her "how to" book, or his father stay up in one of the old garages to iron out a wrinkle in his new *thingamawhatsit* idea. But the house was dead silent at twelve-thirty when he climbed quietly out of bed, got himself assembled with socks, sneakers, purple Wister Wibbles Grammar and Middle School sweatshirt, dark blue (luckily it was midnight blue) jacket, super-sized, best Wister-Wibbles-Hardware-Store, wide-beam, no-fooling flashlight and finally, Putz.

Morris began thinking, a little too late, that he should have gone back out with the Ferdy message as soon as he got it. Now he could only hope Tom had not decided go on one of his little wing-stretching flights. Tom actually had decided that, but Morris caught him just as he was about to take flight, flapping his wings, yawning, and releasing at least a dozen sparks.

"Ooops!" said Tom as soon as he saw Morris racing toward him, dragging Putz, who had wanted to stop and take a leisurely sniff of a bush along the way.

"It was an accident," Tom said. "I won't do it again. Dragon's honor, or whatever!"

"Oh never mind that!" said Morris breathlessly. "Get ready for lift off, Tom. We've got a reply to our ad. It's someone named Ferdy. I've got his address and he's going to be at a window at the back of his house waiting for us. Golly, I never thought we'd actually hear from anyone!" Morris was so excited he could barely get the message out.

"See?" said Tom. "I said the ad was a splendid idea, didn't I? Does he want anything more than just a fly around?"

"I don't know. I reminded him that we do jobs," said Morris. "We'll just have to wait and find out."

"Did you get Ferdy's address?" Tom asked.

"Of course," said Morris "And I can find it. No problem I told him to wait for us at a rear window. It's late, but Policeman Buster might be cruising around, and there's no point in taking chances. But we'd better get started."

"You didn't bring me anything to eat, by any chance, did you?" Tom asked. "I've finished the cornflakes."

"Omigosh!" said Morris. "I forgot all about food. I'm really sorry, Tom. But I don't think we should be late. Do you suppose you can last until we get back? I'll run in then and get you something."

"Besides cornflakes?" asked Tom wistfully. "I liked them, but..."

"Definitely no cornflakes this time," Morris promised.

"Then climb aboard, and let's get going!" said Tom.

So Morris and Putz climbed onto Tom's back and off they flew.

They found 1435 Putty Street with no trouble, and Tom sailed right around to the back of the house. It was a one-story house that looked like dozens of other Wister Wibbles houses, but it did have a high peaked roof with a tall window in it. The window was open, and moonlight fell on someone standing there.

Morris had pretty well convinced himself that Ferdy, whoever he was, probably thought that "*Dragon*" was the name of a car. But you didn't stand in an attic window waiting for a car to drive up. Or perhaps Ferdy just thought someone would stand below and wave up to him. But the person just grinned when Tom flew right up to the window. It was a small boy wearing earmuffs and a jacket over his bathrobe.

"Hello!" he said. "I knew you'd come."

"H-h-hello," stammered Morris. "Are you Ferdy?"

"Yes," said the boy.

"Do you have a computer?" asked Morris.

"Oh yes," said Ferdy. "I've had one since I was five. We do computers in my kindergarten. I'm six now. Are you ready to take me on my dragon ride?"

This was making Morris pretty nervous. It had never occurred to him that Ferdy might be only six.

"I wonder if he asked his mother about this?" Morris whispered to Tom.

"I hope not," said Tom. "Did you consider the consequences if he asked?"

"I know," replied Morris. "But taking a six-year-old on a dragon ride at one in the morning seems pretty risky."

Tom sighed. "Well, go ahead and ask him. But this is all on your head, you know."

"I know," said Morris. "So did you ask your mother if this would be okay, Ferdy?" he asked.

"I don't have a mama anymore," said Ferdy. "Papa's off on another business trip, and there's only Mrs. Dowtwit, who looks after me."

"Well, did you ask *her* then?" said Morris.

"Oh yes," said Ferdy. "But she never believes anything I say, and makes fun of me, especially when Papa's gone."

Tears started to drizzle down Ferdy's cheeks. "She says I have too much 'magination and make things up. She said to go right ahead and take a trip on a dragon if it suits me. So I guess it's all right, isn't it?"

"Will you tell her about it later?" asked Morris.

"Oh yes, I must," said Ferdy. "But she'll just make fun of me. Papa never makes fun of me, though. Not ever. But I think he sometimes agrees with Mrs. Dowtwit about my 'magination. He thinks it's because I'm alone so much. He says one day he's going to get me a dog. But you're not going to say you won't take me on my dragon ride, are you?"

"Certainly not!" said Tom. "Right, Morris?"

"Right!" said Morris.

"Wow!" said Ferdy. "I didn't know dragons could talk."

"This one does," said Tom.

"Come on Ferdy, climb aboard behind me," Morris said. "And hold on tight!"

"Oh, I will," said Ferdy. "Wow!"

"Okay, Tom, we're all set!" said Morris.

"Is Tom my dragon's name?" Ferdy asked.

"You got it," said Morris.

"We're ready for take off, Tom," Ferdy shouted.

And take off they did. Morris kept hearing "Wow!" and "Wow!" behind him as they flew over all the twinkling lights and looked up into the moon and the twinkling stars.

They hadn't been flying long when Tom made a sudden swoop down over Wister Wibbles Park and right over the small Wister Wibbles goldfish pond lit up by the moon, and the reflection of the stars twinkling back at the sky. That's when they saw something thrashing about in the water that definitely wasn't goldfish. Putz began to whine.

"I think there's something in trouble," Morris said. "It might be something that got curious and went off the ledge. Maybe it's a bird or a rabbit. Could we go back and have a closer look, Tom?"

"No problem," said Tom. He made a wide circle, and then swooped down and landed beside the pond where all the splashing was going on. They could see at once it was something larger than a bird or a rabbit. Putz began struggling to leave Morris' arms.

"I think a puppy fell into the water!" Ferdy cried out. "Oh! Oh! Oh! I'm going to rescue him."

"You'll do no such thing," said Morris. "You might fall in and then there would be two of you to rescue. And if you got hurt, Tom doesn't carry dragon travel insurance. Right, Tom?"

"Right, Morris!" said Tom.

"Besides," said Morris, sliding off Tom's back, "I have longer arms than you do, Ferdy. But here, you can hold Putz's leash."

Moments later, as Putz danced excitedly around Ferdy, Morris was cradling a scared, shivering, soaking wet brown puppy in his arms.

"I want to take him home," said Ferdy.

"What will Mrs. Dowtwit say?" asked Morris.

"Oh, I'll just leave him in the attic tonight," Ferdy said quickly. "Tomorrow morning I'll tell her I heard noises up there. I 'spect she'll tell me it's my 'magination. Then she'll make me go up with her and look so then she can tell me 'see, what did I tell you?'"

"What will you tell her when she sees the puppy?" asked Morris.

"I'll tell her I brought him back from my dragon ride," said Ferdy at once. "Then she'll get cross, and tell me she'll speak to Papa about all my nonsense when he gets home tomorrow morning." It appeared that Ferdy had been through these situations several times before.

"But won't she wonder then how the puppy came to be in the attic?" Morris asked.

Ferdy had to take some time for *this* puzzle. His brow winkled as he went into deep thought. "Well," he said finally, "if I leave the window open a bit, I can tell her maybe it's like in fairy tales where witches and goblins leave babies on doorsteps if they want to lose them. I'll tell her I 'spect that's what happened with the puppy. Someone wanted to lose it, so they climbed up a ladder and left it in our attic."

"Will Mrs. Dowtwit believe that?" asked Morris.

"Oh I 'spect she'll get cross again and say where did I hear such a story," replied Ferdy cheerfully.

"And then what will you say?" asked Morris.

"I'll say teacher read it to us in kindergarten," said Ferdy with a wide grin. "So can I take the puppy? I know Papa will let me keep him if we find out he doesn't belong to anybody. I 'spect he doesn't because he doesn't have on a collar. So can I take him home now? Please, please!"

"Well, we can't just leave the puppy here. What do you think, Tom?" Morris asked.

Tom gave a deep, throaty chuckle. "I think anyone who can come up with stories like that ought to have the puppy!"

So moments later, Morris was once again on Tom's back with Putz. Hanging on to him was Ferdy with his flannel bathrobe tightly and warmly wrapped around the puppy. Then back they flew to the upstairs attic window of 1435 Putty Street.

"Will I ever be able to have another dragon ride?" Ferdy asked wistfully as he climbed through the window, hugging the puppy.

"Tom probably has to return to his home," explained Morris. "Right, Tom?"

"Afraid so," said Tom.

"Then I'll never have anyone to tell about my dragon ride," said Ferdy. His eyes welled up with tears again.

"Sure you will," said Morris. "Me! At my e-mail address, putzinapuddle@cork.com, and I'll want to know what happens with the puppy."

"His name is Tomorris," said Ferdy. "That's for Tom and Morris."

"I've never had anything named for me before," said Tom gruffly.

"Me neither," said Morris. "That's cool, Ferdy!"

"If I write, will you answer me?" said Ferdy.

"Of course I will," replied Morris.

"And you won't ever tell me I have too much 'magination?" said Ferdy.

"Never!" replied Morris, who had no imagination at all.

CAUGHT IN THE ACT

Ferdy's dragon ride hadn't really lasted much over an hour, and there was something Morris suddenly decided he wanted to do.

"Would you mind swinging by my father's *thingamawidget* office in the city before we return home?" he asked Tom.

"Why?" asked Tom.

"I don't know," replied Morris. "I just have a feeling I'd like to see it again. It might be a long time before he ever takes me there."

"Couldn't we go tomorrow?" Tom asked.

"What if we get another answer to our ad?" said Morris.

"I hadn't thought of that," said Tom. "But what about my dinner. I hate to say it, but the cornflakes didn't quite do it for me."

"I checked the pantry before I left for school," Morris said. "We have cans and cans of baked beans and tacos and chow mein."

"I know beans, but I don't recognize the other two," said Tom.

"You'll like them, I promise," said Morris.

"Won't opening cans be hard on my teeth?" asked Tom.

"Oh for Pete's sake, Tom, I've already thought of that," said Morris. "I'll bring a can opener and open them all for you. So will you take me? Please!"

"Why not?" said Tom. "But we're going to go at warp dragon speed. So hang on tight to Putz!"

Warp dragon speed was so fast, Morris hardly had time to lose his breath. They arrived at the big building with the golden globe on top in less than one and a half minutes. And it was a good thing they did.

As they pulled up to the office on the top floor, they saw that the moonlight was lighting up more than the big gleaming desk and the leather chairs and the big black safe with the chrome trim. There were two lanterns on the floor next to the big black safe. There were also two men all in black pulling out notebooks and wads of money from the big black safe.

"Does your father come in to work at this hour?" asked Tom.

"That's not my father," said Morris. "Those are crooks trying to steal money and his *thingamawidget* secrets!"

"What can we do about it?" asked Tom.

"I don't know," said Morris "The windows aren't the kind you can open. And... and... and I wouldn't know what to do if we *could* open them. You've forgotten I'm only eleven years old. Maybe we'd better fly back home at warp dragon speed and get my father."

"How are you going to explain me?" asked Tom. "Won't he think I'm, you know, a figment of his imagination?"

"Probably," said Morris, and then thought of something. "But now I have another idea!" He reached into his jacket pocket and pulled out his super-sized, best-Wister-Wibbles-Hardware-Store, wide-beam, no-fooling flashlight.

"I'm going to turn this on and shine it right on you," he said. "They might not know it would take a cannon ball to break these windows. But you start flapping your wings and butting your head against the glass and shooting out sparks. Are you good at sending out flames too?"

"Just watch me!" said Tom.

"Then do it!" said Morris.

Now, it so happened that just as Tom went into his head-butting, flame-shooting act, the door to Morris' father's office opened and a hand reached around the doorframe to switch on a light. Then through the doorway came Pansy in overalls and her head in a pink bandanna, with her bucket, her broom, her mop, and her jaw hanging open. She, of course, was one of the ladies who worked all night cleaning the tall building when it was empty. She had just taken off her glasses to wipe them, so she couldn't see the window where Tom was butting his fierce head against the glass and shooting out flames as scary as Fourth-of-July rockets.

But Pansy could at least see across the room to the big black safe with the chrome trim, and saw the two men, and saw one man frantically nudge the other and point at the window. Then she saw both men drop notebooks and money, grab one lantern, and tear from the room, practically knocking her right off her feet. Without glancing at the window, Pansy went right to the big gleaming desk, and picked up the telephone.

Morris immediately turned off his super-sized, best-Wister-Wibbles-Hardware-Store, wide-beam, no-fooling flashlight.

"What's she doing?" asked Tom.

"I expect she's calling the police," said Morris, which naturally is exactly what Pansy was doing. She sat down in the desk chair, which luckily had its back to the window. She never so much as picked up a single wad of money or even a pencil off the desk to stuff in her overall pocket while she waited for the police to arrive.

"Whew! I guess we can go now," said Morris when the first policeman came charging through the door.

"And get my dinner?" asked Tom.

"And get your dinner," said Morris.

It wasn't until the next evening when his father returned home that he heard all about how two men had somehow found their way into the tall building, and into the office that held the safe where all the *thingamawidget secrets* were kept, not to mention the pots and pots of money.

It seemed to everyone that it must have been Pansy who scared them away. It couldn't have been anything else, even though she insisted all she had with her was her bucket and her broom and mop, and her head in a pink bandana. But it was an undeniable fact that the men ran off when she entered the room. It might have been her pink bandana that scared them away, she thought. But the other undeniable fact was that *she* was the one who then called the police.

Morris' father and the Board of Directors of the company felt Pansy should have a reward for this act, so they were going to give her a nice one. It turned up that Pansy was the sole support of her sister Daisy's three children, not to mention three of her own children (whose father had long since disappeared), Daisy herself, who was crippled, and their two aged parents. So Morris' father and the Board of Directors ended up turning the merely nice reward into an enormous super reward. Then Pansy was promoted to an assistant security guard, and no longer had to lug around a bucket filled with brooms and mops, though she continued to wear her pink bandana because she thought it brought her luck.

Morris had no intention of telling anyone what exactly had happened. It wouldn't have done any good anyway. Who would have believed it? And he was glad that it all had such a happy ending for such a good and honest person as Pansy.

He didn't have much time to think about this, because that very evening, he got another e-mail. It was one that made him really sad, and frightened as well. The request in it had nothing to do with a ride on a dragon. It was an actual job. And even though their ad promised that no job was too big, this one probably was. So what could he really do about it?.

BROWNBERRY@DIDDY.COM

The e-mail was from an address that Morris recognized at once. His mother wrote to it often, and Morris had seen it on a letter or two she had left lying on her desk where she wrote her "how to" books. They were from someone she often wrote to for opinions on one of her new ideas. And the someone was her mother and father, Grampa and Gramma Brinkley.

Grampa and Gramma Brinkley, for some reason, never did send e-mails to Morris, and his sisters. They loved sending cards instead! They sent cards for birthdays, Christmas, Easter, and St. Patrick's Day. They even sent Ground Hog Day cards, graduating from kindergarten, first grade and on up cards, and more often than not, just "thinking-of-you" or "have-a-nice-day" cards. As a result of this, they never bothered to learn the children's e-mail addresses.

Still, they did know the name of his dog, Putz. And so it was curious that they didn't relate it to the e-mail address given in Morris and Tom's *WISTER WIBBLES TIMES* ad.

"Dear owner of Dragon, we have a job for you to do. Please respond promptly. We are desperate. We will write back and tell you how we can meet with you. Also, it is very important that you keep

this letter confidential." They had simply signed their letter, The *Brinkley's.*

Desperate!   Morris' Grampa and Gramma were desperate!

They were desperate enough to be answering an ad in the *WISTER WIBBLES TIMES,* and writing to someone who had a nutty ad that advertised a dragon and would travel. Perhaps it was the *"no job too large"* that did it. But what was the job they wanted done? And how large was it? Why was it they didn't just talk or write to Morris' parents about it?

Grampa and Gramma Brinkley could have moved into the little Wister Wibbles Retirement Home in Wister Wibbles. But they had become all excited by the big, glossy, hip-hop-happy Happy Hills ads that promised them they would be happy forever if they went to live there. It also promised gourmet meals, a swimming pool soon to be built, and lots of fun games and activities to keep them busy and, of course, really, really happy. The little Wister Wibbles Retirement Home only promised they would be comfortable and well taken care of. It was no contest. Comfortable and well taken care of couldn't compete with hip-hop-happy every day where they would be happy forever.

When Morris and his family went to visit them, they could see that the people at Happy Hills never looked as happy as the ads said, including Gramma and Grampa Brinkley. The ones who *did* look happy were Milly and Horace Lovely, who owned Happy Hills. Their pudgy, well-fed, pink faces absolutely spilled over with happiness whenever they greeted visitors. Perhaps Grampa and Gramma just hadn't had time yet to reach the happy state of the ad pictures.

"But it's only a matter of time," the smiling Lovely's assured the Clipper family, "before they know it they will have more happiness than they will know what to do with."

Morris knew he couldn't tell his mother and his father about the e-mail. If he did, he would then have to explain *DRAGON FOR HIRE*. That would open up a whole new bag of worms, or dragons, as it were.

But how was he going to find out why Grampa and Gramma had sent the e-mail without letting *them* know who he was? Maybe once he knew why they had written the letter, and why it was such a secret, then perhaps he could then decide what to do about it. He had to sit and stare at a blank computer screen a long time before he could figure out what to write. This is what he finally did send to Brownberry@diddy.com.

"Dear Brinkley's, Thank you for your interest in our company. As you noted, no job is too large for us, so we are sure we can help you. Please let us know as soon as possible where and when we can meet with you. Thaddeus Q. Putz, DRAGONS, INC. YOUR TRANSPORTATION SERVICE. OTHER JOBS ALSO DONE."

Then he added a *P.S. "If you would like a reference from a satisfied customer, we will be happy to provide it."*

The "satisfied customer" naturally was Ferdy, who was extremely satisfied. Morris hoped Grampa and Gramma wouldn't ask, but he really didn't think they would. A company doesn't tell you to get names of "satisfied customers" if they thought one of them was actually "*dis*satisfied." So why bother? It always sounded good, though.

At first Morris was going to ask the Brinkley's to please get their address to him as soon as possible, more like right away. Then he realized that he didn't really need an address right away, as he already knew where the Happy Hills Home was where his Grampa and Gramma had gone to be happy forever. His idea was that he and Tom would go and float around Happy Hills and see if anything that was happening *outside* might be a clue as what was making his Grampa and Gramma so desperate *inside*.

Then, as it would be the middle of the night, and he happened to know they went to bed right after their favorite T.V. comedy show at ten thirty, he would flash his super-sized Wister-Wibbles-Hardware-Store, wide-beam, no-fooling flashlight in their window to make sure there was nothing suspicious going on inside either.

As he was pretty sure they had no ideas about flying around on a dragon as Ferdy did, he would go by himself after school the following day. There might be no way around it, he would *have* to confess that he was putzeinapuddle@cork.com, and say the dragon was just something he had imagined. Of course, they both knew, like everyone else, that Morris had no imagination, but maybe they would think he had suddenly developed some.

At that point, he would do everything he could to persuade them that if they had a desperate problem, they should tell his mother and his father. After all, anyone who wrote "*how to*" books would surely be able to tell them "*how to*" fix their desperate problem And anyone who had invented anything so complicated as a *thingamawidget*, ought to be able to come up with a solution to just about anything, no matter how desperate it was.

That night, Morris hoped everyone would be in bed and fast asleep before midnight. As it turned out, they all were. And this time he did manage to remember something. He got himself all dressed as usual, and telling Putz he had better "be quiet or else," he crept out to the pantry and loaded a plastic bag with Tom's dinner.

Tom had really liked the tacos and chow mein, so Morris figured he might like to try another exotic foreign food. He dumped two cans of ravioli in the bag. Then he added two cans of spinach. Tom had admitted he was pretty much of a vegetarian and liked his greens, which in his case was mostly edible leaves from the tops of trees. Then Morris got Tom a surprise, two cans of sliced peaches, the sugar-free kind. He had been thinking it wasn't such a hot idea to have given Tom the sugarcoated cornflakes. He certainly didn't want to be responsible for Tom developing dragon-tooth rot.

When he got to the garage, he found Tom outside enjoying a balmy early spring night. He was excited about the choice of food for his dinner, and told Morris he had never eaten fruit in his life. Morris told him he was in for a treat, but asked if he could put off dinner because of a very important flight they had to make. Then he told Tom about the e-mail from his Grampa and Gramma, and how they had gone to Happy Hills to be happy forever, but now it looked as if there might be a big snag regarding the happiness plan.

"It doesn't sound good," Tom said. "What do you propose to do about it?"

Morris explained what he had in mind. There was no doubt that some risk was involved. If they found something really suspicious, what could Morris do about it? Would Grampa and Gramma Brinkley believe him when he reported how he had discovered it? Or would they just report to his mother and his father that his imagination level had gone from zero to 100 million?

Never mind, he would have to take that chance. Tom agreed that he should, and he didn't mind putting off dinner until they got back.

"Canned peaches, eh?" he said. "Excellent!"

So he lifted off at once with Morris and Putz. Putz really seemed to enjoy the flights. The first time he had been trembling almost the whole time, but now he climbed aboard with his tail wagging at top speed. Once settled in front of Morris, he was cool as a canine cucumber, and just as calm. He had no doubt become a seasoned dragon flier.

When they arrived at Happy Hills, they found it plunged in darkness except for a light over the front door. But when Tom flew around to the back of the building, there was a bright light in one of the downstairs windows. It was a surprisingly balmy night, and whoever was in there had raised the window halfway. As Tom slowly drifted past it, Morris looked in. What he saw almost made him plummet right off Tom's back, taking Putz with him.

There was large round table in the middle of the room. On top of it were piles and piles of money. Seated around it were Milly and Hubert Lovely, cheerful owners of Happy Hills. Milly's yellow hair was all done up in curlers, and they were both in matching bright, cheerful yellow bathrobes.

"Please would you park right here?" Morris asked Tom as soon as they'd passed the window. "I want to hear what's going on in there."

Tom glided to a quick stop. Morris slid right off Tom's back with Putz.

"Sit, Putz!" he commanded.

Putz sat.

"Stay, Putz!" said Morris. "Tom, would you please hold on to his leash?"

When Putz's leash had been firmly gripped between Tom's teeth, Morris crept back to the open window. Luckily there was a bush right next to it, so he could peer safely through the leaves into the window. As the Lovely's had no reason to know that anyone was listening to their conversation, they didn't worry a bit about talking as loudly as they pleased.

"Five hundred, Milly!" said Hubert, putting a stack of bills to one side of the table where it joined rows of other stacks.

"Five hundred, Hubert, dear!" Milly said, busily writing this into the notebook.

"Five hundred again, precious," said Hubert picking up another stack.

"Another five hundred!" chirped Milly happily. "Oh, Hubert, dear, this is such fun. Who would ever have thought we could have pulled this off?"

"We couldn't have if there weren't so many gullible simpletons around," said Hubert.

"The old dodos," said Milly. "They actually expect gourmet food. Now, I ask you! Imagine the nerve, complaining to us. Well, we've settled their hash, and put a stop to that, haven't we, sweetness?"

"Oh, that's a clever one, Milly," said Hubert. "Hash! They'd better learn to love it, as that's what they're getting. Gourmet food, ha! Do they think Happy Hills is made of money? Add five hundred more, cuteness."

"Five hundred," said cuteness, entering it in her book. "I wonder when they'll stop asking for entertainment? Sitting in a circle playing pat-a-cake isn't entertaining enough, I suppose. And the old dummies must know by now they're wasting their time wondering when that hole out back is going to become a swimming pool, or when they're actually going to have television in their rooms. That twelve-inch black-and-white T.V. in the parlor is good enough for the lot of them."

"And we owe all this to you, Milly dearest," said Hubert, pausing to come around the table to plant a big kiss on Milly's forehead. It didn't seem to bother him that he missed it and kissed one of her big plastic curlers instead.

"It was your brilliant idea," he went on, "putting that special clause in these contracts in such small letters they look like polka dots." Hubert paused to pick up some sheets of paper from a stack on a desk behind him, and wave them in the air with a huge smile on his round, pink face. "The magnifying glass you need to read it doesn't even exist. Those Clipper's have only another two weeks to find it, and they never will. Nobody else ever has. In two weeks they'll be stuck here for life, like the rest of them. Put down another five hundred, love of my life."

"Oh yes!" said the love of his life, "And every one of them knows it will only get worse for them if they complain to us or anyone else."

"Clever! Clever! Clever!" said Hubert. "Make that another five hundred, lovely one!"

Morris listening at the window was burning up with rage. Those miserable crooks! And his poor Grampa and Gramma scared into pretending to be happy there forever! Morris thought he was going to choke. It seemed there was a clause in the Happy Home contract that would allow them to leave, but they must not know it, just like all the others, because it was in print she size of polka dots.

Well, Morris knew *he* would be able to read it. Didn't he own a Wister-Wibbles-Hardware-Store, super-duper, planetarium-strength, nothing-like-it-in-the-world magnifying glass? If he could just get his hands on that contract, he would find that clause and show it to his Grampa and Gramma before it was too late. He had two weeks left to find it before all was lost. But how was he going to get a copy of that contract? How?!

And then suddenly he knew exactly how. Tom! Hadn't he scared off those burglars from stealing all the *thingamawidget* secrets, not to mention probably piles and piles of money? And who was that sitting not fifteen feet away from him holding Putz's leash in between his teeth? It couldn't be Tom, could it? Ha!

Morris crossed the fifteen feet at dragon warp speed, and quickly explained to Tom that there was something in that room he *had* to have. He had to get those miserable Lovely's out of the room, and so, if he held Putz's leash for a few moments, could Tom please stick his head through the window and take care of that?

"No problem!" said Tom instantly.

"Do you think you could snarl and snap a little? Can dragons do that?" asked Morris. He really wanted to scare the daylights out of those Lovely's.

"You've got to be kidding!" said Tom. "How about a little flame throwing? Should I add a few sparks?"

"Absolutely no flames and sparks," said Morris. "You'll have to control yourself, Tom. Don't forget that Grampa and Gramma live in this building and all those other old people. I just want you to scare the Lovely's out of their wits and out of the room, *not* burn down the building."

"Well, let's get to it," said Tom.

Morris took Putz and crept quietly over to the window. Tom was right behind them. Considering his size and weight, he was amazingly light on his feet. Morris sneaked a quick look into the room, and waved to Tom. Then he ducked down as Tom stuck his head through the window, and began waving it around, snapping and snarling.

There was about three seconds of absolute silence, and then pandemonium broke loose as the Lovely's realized this wasn't a nightmare, but some real, honest-to-goodness, bet-your-bottom-dollar-on-it horrible creature out to get them. And as for bottom dollars, they tried to snatch as many of them as they could in their arms, and went yelling and screaming from the room, sending chairs and lamps crashing to the floor as they went.

Morris lost no time in handing Putz over to Tom's care, and went scrambling over the windowsill. He snatched up several of the contracts he had seen in Hubert Lovely's hands, and wasted not a second scrambling back out again. They were airborne in a moment, and in only a few more moments, were back home again.

As anxious as he was to see what was in those contracts, Morris still took the time to open the cans of ravioli, and spinach, and sliced peaches before he left Tom. Then he left with a promise to be back the next night with maybe, who knew, another answer to their ad, but definitely with news of what he found in the contract, and what he intended to do about it.

Minutes later, he was at his desk with his Wister-Wibbles-Hardware-Store, super-size, planetarium-strength, nothing-like-it-in-the-world magnifying glass in his hand, pouring over the polka dots at the end of a Happy Holiday contract.

Dragon For Hire

THE GREAT HAPPY HOME RESCUE

Morris was going to have to go see Grampa and Gramma at once. He had already decided that he *might* have to do that. After reading those polka dots in the contract, he absolutely *knew* he would have to do it. Unfortunately, he had not figured how to explain everything without getting himself in trouble. If only he had some imagination to draw on. Only he didn't, and that was that. He would just have to wing it. But the point was that Grampa and Gramma were in trouble, *deep* trouble, and what happened to him wasn't nearly as important. He only hoped it wouldn't affect Tom in some way. That would be terrible.

Morris had found an e-mail on his computer from the Browns at Brownberry@diddy.com when he came in from his very enlightening trip to Happy Hills.

"Dear Mr. Thaddeus Q. Putz, it turns out we are not as desperate as we thought. So it looks as if we do not need your Dragon Company services after all. Thank you very much. The Brinkley's. Morris didn't believe this e-mail for a minute. He had no doubt at all that the Lovely's had succeeded in scaring them to death again. Grampa and Gramma were terrified that they would be found out. Well, every time Morris had visited them with his family, hadn't they had to pass by a nasty looking lady at the front desk and tell her what

cheerful residents of Happy Holiday Home they were going to visit? And hadn't the Lovely's always managed to drop by Grampa and Gramma's tiny apartment to spread happiness all over the place? And to think nobody noticed the looks on Grampa and Gramma's faces as they tried to turn unhappy faces into happy faces.

So never mind that e-mail. Morris determined that he was going out there after school armed with his Wister-Wibbles-Hardware-Store, super-size, planetarium-strength, and nothing-like-it-in-the-world magnifying glass and a copy of the contract stuffed in his pocket. He hoped they had their own copy of a contract so he wouldn't have to explain how he got his. But he would if he had to, and that was that.

He had both of these all day with him at school in his lunch bucket. As soon as school was out, he raced to the corner to catch the bus to Happy Holiday Home as it was much too far out of town for him to walk. His heart was thumping hard all the way.

When he arrived at Happy Holiday Home, he didn't go right in, but hung around the glass door, quickly peering in and then ducking away.

Even though that nasty person at the desk didn't appear to be human, she must be. That meant that some time or other she would have to leave the desk. Morris waited and peeked, and waited and peeked. At last, he was rewarded by seeing her stand up, stretch, and disappear down the hallway. To his relief it wasn't the one he had to go down to get to Grampa and Gramma.

Now he only hoped they would be there.

And luckily, they were!

"Why it's Morris! Mercy!" exclaimed his Gramma. "What are you doing here? Is anyone with you?"

"No, Gramma, I'm all by myself. I decided I wanted to see you, so I came on the bus. But please, quick, close the door!" Morris said at once. "They don't know I'm here."

"You mean you were able to sneak past that old bat... "Grampa paused to exchange glances with Gramma. "I mean that lady at the front desk."

"We're so happy to see you. You have no idea!" said Gramma. And she just burst into tears.

Grampa put an arm around her at once. "Whatever made you decide you wanted to see us today," he asked. "You can't imagine how happy we are to see you."

Morris hesitated. He couldn't lie to Grampa and Gramma any more than he could lie to his mother or his father. "I... I'm Thaddeus Q. Putz," he said. "And I didn't believe you when you said you weren't desperate anymore."

"You're *WHO*?" asked Grampa.

"Thaddeus Q. Putz," said Morris. "I'm surprised you didn't recognize Putz's name, but I'm glad you didn't. I think you really are desperate, and I wanted to see if I could help."

"Oh, think of that, dear," said Gramma. "This lovely child has come to help us. But there's really nothing you or anyone can do."

"The fact is, man to man," said Grampa, putting a hand on Morris' shoulder, "we're stuck here and we don't like it. Happy, my aching eyebrow! Nobody is happy here but the dear Lovely's. Nothing is what the ads say it is. They tell us that if we complain, they'll only make it worse for us. And the truth is we've put all our money into this place, and can't afford to go anyplace else."

"I'll bet my father would help," said Morris.

"We wouldn't let him if he wanted to," said Grampa. "He and your dear mother tried to persuade us to go the Wister Wibbles Retirement Home where we would not only be comfortable and well taken care of, but nearer you as well. But we thought we knew more than they did, and fell for all that happy forever nonsense. Nobody can be happy forever, Morris. Don't you forget that."

Now Grampa's eyes welled with tears.

"But why can't you get your money back?" Morris asked.

"It's in the contract," said Grampa sadly. "We've pored over it and pored over it to see if there's some way out of it. But we're stuck. And that's that."

"Could I see the contract?" Morris asked. "Do... do you have a copy?" He was keeping his fingers crossed.

"Yes," replied Grampa. "But you're only eleven, Morris. I'm afraid contracts might be a bit difficult for you to understand."

"I'd like to try," said Morris. "Please?"

"Let him," said Gramma. "It won't hurt anything."

Grampa didn't have to look far for the contract. It was sitting right on their little desk, the one with the computer on it. Morris was glad that the Lovely's at least had allowed them even to *have* one. They probably just hadn't thought yet about it.

The contract Grampa handed Morris was all wrinkled and worn from having been read and re-read.

Morris pretended he'd never seen it before, and sat there pretending to read it carefully. But when he got to the end of the contract to where the little black dots were, he reached into his pocket and pulled out his Wister-Wibbles Hardware Store, super-size, planetarium-strength, nothing-like-it-in-the-world magnifying glass.

"Do you always carry that thing around with you?" asked Grampa.

"Not always," replied Morris. "Just when I think I might need it."

"What made you think you would need it today?" asked Grampa.

"Because you said you were desperate, and you never know," said Morris.

"That's very true," said Grampa. "But I don't know how a magnifying glass is going to find something that isn't there."

"That's true, too, Grampa. But it turns out there *is* something there. Here, look!" Morris handed him the contract and the magnifying glass, and pointed to the little black dots. "You and Gramma read that," he said.

So Grampa, with Gramma hanging over his shoulder, looked through the magnifying glass and read the little black dots, which weren't really dots at all.

"After three months, if you don't believe that you will be happy forever at Happy Hills, your money in its entirety, minus fifty-dollar processing fees, will be cheerfully refunded."

First Grampa read it to himself. Then, as if he couldn't really believe it, had to read it out loud to Morris, who of course had already read it. Several times.

"Omigosh! Omigosh! Omigosh!" said Grampa.

"Oh my!" said Gramma. "But can they make us say we think we will be happy forever, if we don't think that?"

"Absolutely not!" said Grampa. "They can't make us say anything we don't want to. Not ever again!"

"And now you'll tell father and mother, won't you?" asked Morris.

"Oh absolutely!" said Grampa, looking as if he was going to explode with happiness.

"But... but," Morris hesitated. "Are you going to have to tell them about putzinapuddle@cork.com?

"Don't you want us to?" asked Grampa.

"Not if you don't have to," said Morris. "Could you please just say you finally found the polka dots in the contract?"

"Absolutely," said Grampa. "And it's the truth. We finally did. Our lips will be sealed. Isn't that right, old girl?'

"Right!" agreed Gramma with a huge, enormous smile.

"But would you like to explain something to me?" asked Grampa. "What is all this thing about *DRAGON FOR HIRE*? Is it a business you're going into, sort of doing odd jobs for people?"

"Sort of," said Morris.

"You know, Morris," said Grampa, "I had a business when I was your age. I was collecting earthworms to *sort of sell* on a street stand in the summer. You know, instead of lemonade. I was storing them in a jar in the refrigerator. I *sort of* didn't want my mother to know they were there. She wasn't too happy when she found them accidentally one day."

"I don't see what earthworms have to do with Morris' dragon," said Gramma.

"Oh I don't know," said Grampa. "I just *sort of had* a funny idea that they might." And he gave Morris a big wink.

POLLYH@KITKAT.COM & DICKYF@KITKAT.COM

When he arrived home from his visit to Grampa and Gramma at Happy Hills, Morris found two e-mails waiting for him. The dragon business was really booming. Morris had trouble believing how successful his ad was. Tom already had enough to report to Old Pew to earn him a pile of dragon points. Now here were two more. The only problem was that they sounded suspiciously as if Ferdy had been in touch with his kindergarten friends. But that didn't really matter. Old Pew would accept dragon deeds even if they were only performed for six-year olds.

The first e-mail was from PollyH@kitkat.com, and the second was from DickyF@kitkat.com. Both of them did sound more grown up than Ferdy's letter, but perhaps they had some help writing them, probably from someone who didn't believe Ferdy's tale for a moment.

Polly wrote: *"I am interested in your dragon rides. I expect you must give them late at night because that is when dragons are out. If you are free to give one tonight, please write me back right away I will be ready at midnight. My address is 2995 Pansy Drive. Thank you. Polly H."*

Dicky wrote: *"I believe you offer dragon rides. If you really do, I am free at midnight tonight. Let me know at once if this is okay, and I will be ready and waiting. My address is 387 Dipsy Avenue. Thanks. Dicky F."*

So far, the only passengers Tom had transported were Morris and Putz, and then Morris, Putz, and Ferdy. But Morris believed that Tom could easily carry himself, Putz and two six-year-olds. Probably more than that even, if push came to shove.

So Morris wrote the same letter to both Polly H. and Dicky F.

"The Dragon is free tonight for rides and will be happy to pick you up a half hour past midnight. Be waiting at a window in the back of your house. An upstairs window if you have one is best. Please wear a warm jacket and earmuffs. Thank you. Thaddeus Q. Putz, DRAGONS, INC. YOUR TRANSPORTATION SERVICE. OTHER JOBS ALSO DONE."

Morris continued to feel it didn't hurt to go on letting people know about other jobs. After all, that's how he learned about Grampa and Gramma's desperate situation.

Once again, he hoped nobody in the family was planning to be up late. Nobody was, and when he heard the grandfather clock bonging eleven and a half times, the house was already dark and silent.

Morris had managed to sneak Tom's dinner out of the pantry earlier, so had a sack already filled with two cans of spaghetti o's, two jars of peanut butter to be eaten together with two boxes of healthy whole wheat crackers, and, by special request, two more cans of sliced peaches.

"I'm going to be the healthiest dragon who ever lived," Tom said.

"That's the idea," replied Morris. "Are you about ready to take off?"

"I'll save some of this until I get back," Tom said. "Two six-year-olds won't keep us out long. But that's two more deeds to add to my list. Old Pew will be impressed. Come on, let's get going."

Morris felt that he would never get over being excited climbing aboard Tom with Putz, and sailing off into the night. Even if tonight they were only taking a couple of six-year-old kids on a ride, he didn't care. After all, you couldn't have a big adventure every time, and if nothing else, this added two more deeds that Tom could report to Old Pew.

Morris wasn't sure of either of the addresses they were going to, but they soon found the first one, Polly H's house at 2995 Pansy Drive. It was a pretty little English cottage with a peaked roof just like the kind on Ferdy's house. As Morris had asked Polly to be at a back window, upstairs preferred, Tom flew right around to the back. They saw at once that Ferdy's little six-year old friend, was already standing there, waiting.

The surprise was that while Polly appeared to have on a jacket, a big puffy light blue one, as well as earmuffs, she also appeared to be taller than Ferdy. Much, much taller! And when they drew right up beside the window for Polly to climb on, Morris saw that it definitely was NOT someone six years old. She was someone older. Much, much older! When he saw who it was, Morris barely managed to keep himself from sliding right off Tom's back.

"Woof!" said Putz anxiously.

Morris quickly pulled himself back. "G-g-g-good evening, m-m-m-madam!"

"Good evening," said the much older Polly. "You are right on time. Should I climb on?"

"Please do," said Tom.

"A-a-a-and you m-m-m-may hang on to me," said Morris.

The much older Polly put one leg up and slid onto Tom's back behind Morris. Then Morris felt her arms fasten around his waist.

"We're picking someone else up," Tom said as they took off. "I hope you don't mind."

"Oh, not at all!" said the much older Polly cheerfully. Then she shouted into Morris' right ear. "You know, young man, you look very much like someone I know."

"Well, I don't believe I am," said Morris. And, of course he was telling a big, fat, big-as-a-hot-air-balloon, no-question-about-it, huge, enormous lie.

For he knew that he not only probably *looked* like someone Polly H. knew, but he actually *was* someone she knew. Because he knew almost at once what the H. in Polly H. stood for. Yes, Polly H. was no other than his real, honest-to-goodness, bet-your-bottom-dollar-on-it fifth-grade teacher Miss Picklesticker!

Miss Picklesticker sitting on Tom's back with her arms clasped around him while they went to pick up their second passenger!

Their second passenger! Oh no! Morris suddenly had the terrible feeling he knew who it could be. Had they planned this? Or, if he was right about what he was thinking, was she just in for one grand, enormous, fall-right-off-a-dragon's-back surprise?

Morris was holding his breath as they pulled up to the back of the second house. He had the answer to his question in an instant. He couldn't see her face behind him, but he could hear Miss Picklesticker gasp.

"Oh my goodness!" she breathed in his ear. If that wasn't a surprised "oh my goodness," then Morris had never heard one.

Standing in his upstairs window was not a little Dicky F. but none other than a tall Mr. Dicky Fostersill, Morris' mathematics teacher at Wister Wibbles Grammar and Middle School, complete with navy blue sailor's P-jacket (from his navy days), and red earmuffs.

"Good-good-good evening Mr. Fostersill!" stammered Miss Picklesticker.

"Good-good-good-good evening, Miss Picklesticker!" stammered Mr. Fostersill.

"May I join you?" asked Mr. Fostersill.

"Please do," said Miss Picklesticker.

"Should I sit behind Miss Picklesticker?" asked Mr. Fostersill.

"Oh, yes," said Morris quickly. He didn't fancy sitting sandwiched between his two Wister Wibbles Grammar and Middle School teachers. It was bad enough having

Miss Picklesticker clasping him around the waist. Anyway, Mr. Fostersill in front of him would obstruct his and Putz's view.

Tom hovered outside the window as Mr. Fostersill climbed aboard.

"May I hang on to you, Miss Picklesticker?" he asked.

"Please do," said Miss Picklesticker.

"He'll fall off if he doesn't," snapped Tom, who had very sharp hearing.

Because they were now sitting so close together, Morris could feel that Mr. Fostersill now had clasped Miss Picklesticker around the waist. Morris was trying to breathe normally as he pictured this going on behind him.

"Where would you two like to go?" Tom said as he hovered outside the window.

"Do you mean we can choose?" Mr. Fostersill asked.

"Certainly," said Tom.

"Oh my!" exclaimed Miss Picklesticker. "I've always wanted to go to the North Pole. My dear departed Uncle Cicero was a North Pole explorer. But he refused to wear his warm flannel underwear. The stubborn creature froze to death in an igloo before he ever had the chance to keep his promise to take me there one day."

"Well, I've always wanted to go to a forest in South America," said Mr. Fostersill. "My Aunt Delicia went there to save alligators from being collected by alligator bag makers. But the stubborn creature refused to believe she should be careful around them. She ended up being collected by one herself before she kept her promise to let me accompany her one day."

Then Miss Picklesticker giggled. "But aren't we being silly, Mr. Fostersill. The North Pole and South America! That would take days."

Mr. Fostersill chuckled. "Months!"

"Minutes!" snapped Tom. "I can take you both places in minutes at quadruple warp dragon speed. Is that seriously what you'd both like to do?"

"Wouldn't we Miss Picklesticker?" asked Mr. Fostersill.

"Of course, Mr. Fostersill," replied Miss Picklesticker.

"Please, Miss Picklesticker, won't you call me Dicky?" asked Mr. Fostersill. "We'll be traveling together for some time it seems, even at quadruple warp dragon speed."

"Why...why...yes...D-d-d-Dicky," stammered. Miss Picklesticker. "If you... you will call me Polly."

"I'd be delighted... P-p-p-Polly," stammered back Mr. Fostersill.

To Morris, sitting in front of them, it felt suspiciously as if Mr. Fostersill's arms had tightened around Miss Picklesticker's waist.

"Well, now that we have that settled," said Tom. "We're off!"

And off they were to the North Pole. They arrived there in an amazing twenty minutes. Soon they were looking down on icebergs, polar bears, and igloos.

"I wonder if..." said Miss Picklesticker.

"Don't even think about it, Polly dear," said Mr. Fostersill.

Morris was sure the arms tightened still further around Miss Picklesticker's waist.

Then after they had done a final spin over the North Pole, they flew down to the Amazon forest in South America, and saw alligators sunning themselves on the banks of the Amazon River.

"I wonder if..." said Mr. Fostersill.

"Don't even think about it, Dicky, dear," said Miss Picklesticker.

Morris felt one of Miss Picklesticker's arms briefly (and dangerously, he felt) leave his waist. He supposed it might be more than likely because the hand attached to the arm was squeezing Mr. Fostersill's hand attached to the arm around *her* waist.

While they were sailing over the Amazon forest, Morris heard Mr. Fostersill whisper to Miss Picklesticker, "By the way, Polly, dear, don't you think our young dragon owner looks suspiciously like one of our students at Wister Wibbles Grammar and Middle School."

"Oh, I suggested to him that he might be someone I know," said Miss Picklesticker. "But he says he doesn't believe he is. I thought he looked like the boy in my class who is sadly lacking in imagination."

"I'm afraid I don't have any either, Polly dearest," said Mr. Fostersill. "You know it never has taken imagination to add up two and two. If one of my students imagines something other than four, I must give them an F for failure."

"Of course, you must, Dicky, my love," said Miss Picklesticker. "We will never say more about it. At any rate, I believe our young owner of the dragon business is Thaddeus Q. Putz just as he says he is. Oh, and here we are arriving at my house!"

Morris felt an extra squeeze going on behind him as Mr. Fostersill released his arm from around Miss Picklesticker's waist.

"Until we meet again, Polly dear!" Morris heard Mr. Fostersill whisper.

Morris, in thinking all this over, wondered just how much imagination it would take for him to forget all this carrying on and get some winks of sleep the remaining hours until morning.

Dragon For Hire

IMAGINATION

"Oh, they'll just think they dreamed the whole thing," Tom said to Morris when they arrived home. He was chomping on the crackers and peanut butter and picking his teeth with his claw as he and Morris were having a brief review of the evening in the garage.

"I don't know," Morris said. "I don't think Ferdy believes he dreamed *his* ride."

"Ferdy's six years old," said Tom.

"But whose dream was it," asked Morris. "Miss Picklesticker's or Mr. Fostersill's."

"Ah!" said Tom. "That's the ten-million-dragon-dollar question. I suppose you'll find out at school this morning."

Morris didn't suppose any such thing, but he *did* notice something pretty unusual right away. It was Thursday, Miss Picklesticker's day for her green dress with the lace collar and cuffs. Only she was wearing her grey dress with the blue roses on it, strictly her MWF dress.

Morris had no idea why he ever noticed such things, but the fact was that he did. It didn't take imagination, just keen powers of observation, which it appeared that he had.

Well, along with his ability to add two and two and always have it turn out four. It was curious to him that nobody else seemed to notice this rare event, or another one.

Mr. Fostersill, despite the fact that he wasn't exactly the youngest apple on the Wister Wibbles Grammar and Middle School tree, was an assistant to the assistant to the assistant soccer coach. He often appeared in the classroom first thing in the morning to announce that soccer practice would be cancelled, or moved to another time, or whatever somebody had told him to announce. The class was used to his coming in with his ratty old grey sweater, practically out at the elbows.

"Beg pardon, Miss Picklesticker," he would say. "May I interrupt to make an announcement?"

"Of course, Mr. Fostersill," Miss Picklesticker would reply.

This had gone on as long as anyone could remember. It was probably going on when Morris' father and mother had been fifth graders at Wister Wibbles Grammar and Middle School. Today Mr. Fostersill appeared in a new grey sweater that Morris noticed still had the tag dangling from one sleeve cuff. It was probably a Christmas present that had never left the box.

Today, as usual, though, hardly anyone paid any attention when Mr. Fostersill entered the classroom.

"Beg pardon," said Mr. Fostersill. There was a long, long pause during which he turned a bright pink. Then he added, "Polly."

"Of course," said Miss Picklesticker, who turned an even brighter pink. Then she added, "Dicky."

At this point, you could almost hear the collective jaws of the entire fifth grade drop. Miss Picklesticker immediately turned her back to the class to write the English assignment on the blackboard. By the time she turned around again, she had somehow managed to de-pink her cheeks and was the same Miss Picklesticker the fifth grade was used to.

"I believe, we will once more try to stre-e-e-etch our imaginations," she said. Out flew her thin arms again. "I will expect a story or essay by next Monday."

Morris wished he could write something really spectacular this time. But the only thing he could think of was cornflakes again. He wished... he wished... he wished... but no, he didn't dare. Anyway, he had something much more important to think about than wanting to impress Miss Picklesticker.

He reported to Tom what had happened in the classroom that day. Then Tom took Morris for one final flight. Final, because he was leaving the next night.

Tom had casually mentioned when he was picking peanut butter from his teeth with a claw that the last night might really be his last one. He had said when they got back from the North Pole and the Amazon forest in South America that what he had done probably would do it for Old Pew.

"So I've done four deeds, haven't I?" Tom said. "At the very least."

Morris had to admit that he had.

There was Ferdy. There was scaring off the burglars at Morris' father's *thingamawidget* office. There was scaring off the Lovely's so Morris could filch the contract for his Grampa and Gramma. And finally there was fulfilling the practically lifelong wishes of two people to visit the North Pole and the Amazon forest. That last really ought to be counted as two deeds. Maybe even four when you took into account that a flight on Tom the dragon had finally caused romance to bloom and brought them together after all these years. Right? That made, all told five good solid deeds. If Old Pew wasn't impressed with that, what in all of this dragon's world *would* impress him?

Besides, didn't you say the garage fix-it man was coming the next day to fix the garage door?" Tom asked.

"He might not," said Morris.

"Well, I'm not going to go looking for another place to hang out, or another boy to hang out with, if that's what you think," Tom said. "I'll never find another boy I'll like as much as you, Morris. Besides, I don't think I could ever find anyone with absolutely no imagination who doesn't believe I'm a figment of one."

"I don't see how anyone would believe you're not a dragon," said Morris. "All you have to do is breathe a few sparks to prove it."

"Not interested," said Tom.

Of course, Morris didn't want Tom to be somebody else's dragon. Not ever. He was glad that Tom didn't want that either.

"Do... do you think I'll ever see you again?" he asked.

"Nobody ever knows what's just around the corner, or coming out of mountain caves," Tom said. "Let's not even think about it."

"Maybe dragons will get computers one day, and you can write me," said Morris. "*Putzinapuddle@cork.com*. Try to remember it."

"I will," said Tom. "Now run along to bed. Let's not get sloppy over this."

"Okay," Morris said. He reached out and patted Tom on his soft back.

Tom gave him a nudge with his snout. He'd never done that before.

But there was one more thing that bothered Morris. He wished his sisters Belinda and Clorinda could have known Tom and had a flight on him. That morning at breakfast, he decided he would break down and ask them if they would like one. Then he'd always have someone to talk it all over with.

"Don't be an idiot," said Belinda

"You're being silly," said Clorinda.

"Just thought I'd ask," said Morris.

"I think you may finally be developing an imagination," said Belinda.

"Wheee!" said Clorinda, who really knew nothing at all about it.

So that was that. And it was just as well they hadn't said "yes." The fix-it man never did show up, so Morris took

Putz and crept out to the garage in the middle of the night with another sack of all the things Tom liked best, just in case. But Tom was gone. All that was left was the faint smell of cinnamon and nutmeg.

* * * *

That weekend Morris wandered around doing nothing. Or he sat in front of his computer and stared at the blank screen. Or he sat in a chair staring into space. If only he had some imagination, he could imagine Tom back, but he hadn't and he couldn't.

He tried to think of all the people he and Tom had made happy.

Ferdy would have his dragon ride to remember forever, and a puppy as well. Morris had already gotten an e-mail from Ferdy@kitkat.com. "Dear Morris and Tom, my puppy has no home so Papa says I can keep him. Your friend, Ferdy."

Morris and Tom had saved his father's *thingamawidget* secrets and pots of money from being stolen.

Because of Morris and Tom, Pansy with her pink bandana, her crippled sister, three plus three children, and their aged parents all would have happier lives.

Grampa and Gramma had bid the dear Lovely pair farewell, and already packed and moved to the Wister Wibbles Retirement Home. There, Gramma was allowed to have her white enamel table in their kitchen and roll out piecrust any time she felt like it. Never mind about being happy forever, Grampa and Gramma said. They were content just being comfortable and taken care of, although *that* in the end made them about as happy as anybody could be.

Polly and Dicky, otherwise known as Miss Picklesticker and Mr. Fostersill, had at long last not only finally discovered what it was to visit the North Pole and the Amazon Forest, but had at long last discovered each other as well.

Morris had nothing left himself but the memory of Tom, and only the very faint smell of cinnamon and nutmeg in the garage. After the garage was cleared out for the great yard sale, even the smell would be gone.

Now he had to sit down and stre-e-e-etch his imagination, of which he still had none, for Miss Picklesticker. And he would have to do it by Monday. He wondered if could get away with writing about cornflakes again. He sat and stared and stared into space, and finally, at long last, he decided something.

He went to his computer and started writing. He wrote and he wrote. When he finally finished, he printed out what he had written, stuffed it in his school bag, put the leash on Putz, and went for a long walk. And then he began to think that Tom *had* left him something besides just a memory. He could visit Grampa and Gramma who were now close enough in Wister Wibbles that he could walk there with Putz. Wister Wibbles Retirement Home loved dogs, so Putz was always welcome there as well.

"Maybe he'll come back one day," Morris said, "Maybe Old Pew will give him some more tasks to do. What do you think, Putz?"

"Woof!" said Putz.

And Morris, who had no imagination, imagined that "woof" definitely meant "yes!"

EPILOGUE

The following Monday night Miss Picklesticker sat at *her* desk reading all the papers that had been turned in by her fifth grade. She was very, very discouraged. Nobody had really stre-e-e-etched. In front of her was her special pen with the bright purple ink that she used *only* for that one paper she felt deserved an A plus. The last time, for the first time ever, she had been able to use it twice.

This time even Mortimer Quintillius Gable and Serena Sophronia Gerard had let her down. Mortimer wrote about how he had a toothache and had to visit the dentist. He seemed to think mentioning the word "spit" several times showed imagination. Serena wrote about how her dog pooped all over her bed and simply *ruined* her nice new bedspread. Miss Picklesticker was inclined to think they were both trying to be humorous, but she did not think "spit" and "poop" were particularly humorous. And she wasn't sure where imagination came into all this. She passed up both papers with a sigh.

She finally came to the last paper, and sighed even further when she saw who the author was. If *this* one showed any imagination, she would go out and dance in the street. It was pretty safe to say she would never have to do that. She began to read. And this is what Miss Picklesticker read:

"One night I decided to go into the garage and find something I had begun to think a lot about. The door was busted (Miss Picklesticker paused to cross that out and put in "broken") and I was afraid it would be lost or stolen. What I found there was something nobody would probably ever believe. But these are all the things that happened because of what I found in the garage that night. It was a dragon, and his name was Tom."

Miss Picklesticker read and read without stopping until she got to the very end. When she had finished, she knew she could never actually do anything as foolish as dancing in the street. She also knew that she could never even hang this on the bulletin board. Oh, it wasn't because she wouldn't want to. It was because she knew the person who wrote it would not want her to.

The person would probably not want anybody but Miss Picklesticker herself to know anything about what she had read. But there *was* something she *could* do. A slow smile crossed her face, as she finally picked up her pen with the special bright purple ink.

This is the author's first book featuring a dragon, about which she claims to know very little, but has gone ahead and written this book anyway, with apologies to all if the dragon doesn't quite fit what everyone's idea of a dragon ought to be.

www.ingramcontent.com/pod-product-compliance
Lightning Source LLC
Chambersburg PA
CBHW031843170626
46807CB00004B/1599